HOW TO COMMIT MURDER AND GET AWAY WITH IT

HOW TO COMMIT MURDER AND GET AWAY WITH IT

A Novel

Diego

iUniverse, Inc.
New York Lincoln Shanghai

HOW TO COMMIT MURDER AND GET AWAY WITH IT

iUniverse books may be ordered through booksellers or by contacting:

iUniverse
2021 Pine Lake Road, Suite 100
Lincoln, NE 68512
www.iuniverse.com
1-800-Authors (1-800-288-4677)

Because of the dynamic nature of the Internet, any Web addresses or links contained in this book may have changed since publication and may no longer be valid.

This is a work of fiction. All of the characters, names, incidents, organizations, and dialogue in this novel are either the products of the author's imagination or are used fictitiously.

ISBN: 978-0-595-47809-5

Printed in the United States of America

The Murder

Cheryl hung up the phone. She looked around her apartment almost in disbelief. The day after tomorrow she would be gone—back home with her parents in Howells. She had just given her mother her flight arrangements to Phoenix. Saturday. She arrives on Saturday. It was almost surreal. Last week she was working as an intern and making love to the man she loved and this week she's on her way back home. Cliff. What was she going to do without seeing Cliff everyday? Would she really get a job in Phoenix? How was she going to make love to Cliff while she was living with her parents? Cliff said it would be alright. They'd find a way to be together when he came back to visit with his constituents—which he promised to do more often than he had been over the past two years.

She sat on her overstuffed chair and looked carefully at her efficiency apartment. A kitchen with a dining table, a bathroom and the sofa that pops out into a bed. She remembers the first time she and Cliff made love on the bed. He stopped by after one of the many State Dinners he attended. He smelled like liquor but he was so powerful, so focused, focused on her. It all happened so quickly. He was in her door and before she knew it, he was in her mouth. He was an animal. Nothing else existed except him. She was hot. He was bigger than she had ever expected. It was amazing. They never did open the bed that night. He made love to every orifice of her body.

How many times had they made love since then? It seemed like a thousand but she'd only been here for less than two years, so how could it be? Whatever it was, it wasn't enough. She wanted to see him before she left. He said he couldn't. His wife was in Washington all week. But he said he'd send word if he could get away.

There was a knock at her door. She was startled. Could it be Cliff? She looked out the small window next to the door. No, it's not. It's some guy in a uniform. Maybe he's sending word.

She opened the door with the security latch on. "Cheryl Chapin?" the uniformed man asked.

"Yes, I'm Cheryl."

"I have a message from Representative Lewis. May I come in?"

Oh my God, I *am* going to see him before I leave, she thought.

"Yes. Yes, please come in."

Cheryl closed the door and unlocked the security lock. She opened up the door. The uniformed man was standing completely still. Like he was guarding the Tomb of the Unknown Soldier or, maybe, completely bored. I guess he doesn't know how exciting this is, she thought.

He came in and closed the door behind him, softly.

She was flustered. Too excited to just stand there.

"Can I get you something to drink?" she asked.

"Ma'am." He said with a nod.

Cheryl turned towards the kitchen on the right; Staff Sergeant Anthony Malone lunged, leading with his left hand until it was around the right side of her face. His right hand was in place on the upper part of the back of her head. Staff Sergeant Malone finished this one lunging movement by pulling her chin back towards him with his left hand and pushing slightly downward with his right hand. He stepped back.

Cheryl was dead before her body hit the floor.

The Victim

10 days earlier

Cheryl Chapin entered the doors to the Department of the Interstate Commerce Commission as she had done every Monday for almost two years. Monday again. Cheryl hated Mondays. She had to finish up the report for last week and then there was the staff meeting where she would get her assignment for the week and the cycle would start again. She'd seen it so many times before, if only this week could be different.

"Cheryl!" It was Maria. Maria del Carmen Morales. But she hated the "del Carmen" part, so all of her friends just called her Maria Morales. "Cheryl. How was your weekend?"

"I am so tired; I'm glad it's Monday so I can sleep during staff."

"Pinche!, I'm so jealous. Why can't I meet a man who sweeps me off my feet and I'll never know when I touch ground again. You are so lucky. Let's get some coffee."

Cheryl finished her report and headed for the staff meeting. The meeting is made up of the interns in the Department; herself, Maria from California, Brian Cooper from Pennsylvania and Laura Miller from Ohio. Then there were the staff members; Mark Turner who had been here for more administrations than anyone cared to remember, Sophie Harding who was new with this administration and still had the fire in her eyes—as if the fate of interstate commerce was going to be the deciding factor in the success of the administration and democracy as a whole, Jon Peters and Willa Russo who were both holding on by a thread from the previous administration and, of course, the department manager, Robert Williams III. They called him Bob. He hated Bob. "My name is Robert Williams the 3rd. It was good enough for my father and grandfather, so I'll thank you to respect their memory and use the name that they gave me."

"Lighten up, Bob. With no disrespect, there's a time that you can be Robert Williams the 3rd and a time that you can be Bob."

"I disagree. If Dad had wanted a "Bob", he would have named me 'Bob'."

"Come on, Bob."

"I don't respond to 'Bob'. I'll 'bob and weave' and I'll even 'bob for apples' on occasion, but I will not respond to 'Bob'".

The meeting was a déjà vu experience of last week and the week before. As they were leaving, she heard Laura talking to Bob. "It's official; I'll be graduating this May. I was hoping that I could extend my education for another semester. But, it is what it is."

"We're going to miss you." Robert responded. "Cheryl." Bob caught her as she was leaving the door. "Aren't you graduating this May also?"

"Afraid so, Bob."

"What are you doing for your senior project?" Asked Laura.

"Oh, I've already finished it. I met my requirements to graduate in December, but I'm waiting for May to walk, so I can party hardier."

"You've graduated?" Robert was incredulous.

"Well, no. Maybe"

"It doesn't matter about the ceremony, if you've completed your school you can't be here."

"What?"

"Meet me in my office."

Twenty minutes and two phone calls later and it was official. Her last day in the office would be next Friday; barely meeting the two week notice requirement of all government jobs. How could this happen? Why? What a ridiculous rule. She hadn't graduated yet. Leave it to Bob to be so anal retentive about the rules. He had checked with the Human Resources Department of the Interstate Commerce Commission and then called the Attorney Generals' Office for a final opinion on the statute regarding intern job placement. What a loser. Who would have noticed? Who would have cared if she remained lost in the bureaucracy somewhere in Washington D.C.?

"Maria, I'm fucked."

"I hear about it every Monday. That's why I come to work."

"No, I mean it. Bob just fired me."

"What? How?"

"He says that I've graduated and I can't work as an intern any more. Next Friday is my last day."

"Oh, God. What are you going to do?"

"I don't know."

"What about your stud? Can't you get a job on his staff?"

"Maria, shhh. No, I can't get a job on his staff. I've already asked and he said that we would be too close and he wouldn't be able to explain the change to his wife."

"What kind a leash does she keep on him, anyway?"

"Apparently, pretty tight. He's fed up with her but he's waiting until after re-elections before he does anything. Anyway, that's a non-starter."

"Can't he pull some strings … help you out? I'm sure he can."

"I'll ask. I'm not giving up hope, yet."

Cheryl spent the rest of the day reliving the nightmare that had taken place in Bob's office. Why was he such an asshole? Why had she been so smug with Laura to begin with. Over and over she played the scene in her head until there was nothing else happening.

"Hey, are you going home? Or are you going to do your last two weeks in consecutive shifts and be done this weekend?"

"Hey Maria. No, I'm out of here. Thanks for waking me up."

"You weren't sleeping."

"No, I'm just a little shocked from today."

"Well, you just get a hold of that man and he'll make things right."

"I hope so."

Cheryl was calling Cliff's office for the twelfth time. The first two she had talked with Barb. Barbara Gomez was a good friend and was on Cliff's staff. It was Barb who introduced Cheryl to Cliff. After all, she was an intern from his district and Barb kept at him until Cliff finally found time in his schedule to meet with Cheryl. It was exciting to meet with an actual Representative of the United States government. He was so powerful. He was one of the few hundred men who directed the most powerful country in the world. And here she was shaking his hand, having her picture taken with his arm around her waist. It seemed almost surreal. And then it was over. She went back to work and continued learning her new job with the Interstate Commerce Commission. Two weeks later, she received a call at home.

"Cheryl Chapin?"

"Yes, this is Cheryl."

"Cheryl, this is Representative Lewis. I don't know if you remember, but we met in my office."

"Yes, yes sir, of … of course I remember."

"I was calling to see if we could continue the discussion we started that day."

Discussion? "Yes, of course."

"Great. Look, I've got a State Dinner to attend, but I was hoping after that I could stop by your place."

"Um, sure … sure, no problem. Um, I don't know what to say."

"Just give me your address and we'll talk this evening."

"Oh yeah, of course. It's 1482 New York Avenue. Apartment J."

"Thanks, see you soon."

Her heart was racing. What had just happened? Was she completely out of it? There was a discussion? She didn't remember any discussion. What was she going to do? What was she going to say? She'd look like a moron if she didn't know what the Representative wanted to talk to her about.

Maybe she should call Barb, She might remember the conversation. Or maybe he's thinking of a conversation with someone else. Barb would know.

"No, bad idea." She didn't know why, but she just felt that the fewer people who know about this, the better.

She took a shower and got dressed. Unsure of what might happen, but excited at the thought of Representative Cliff Lewis coming to talk with intern Cheryl Chapin, Cheryl couldn't help but put on a little make-up.

Hours later came the knock on the door. Immediately, her heart was racing again. How would she ever get through the night in this condition? How was she going to carry on a conversation with her heart in her throat?

She opened the door. Representative Lewis smiled and stepped forward to walk in. She stepped to the side as he came into her little place. It was as if she had stepped into a shower of self-consciousness and embarrassment as he glanced around the room.

"Nice place you've got here."

He likes it. "Thanks. I'm still settling in, but I think like it." She got her first whiff of liquor on his breath.

"It's very warm and tender, just like you." He held out his hand.

Without a thought, she extended her hand into his. He pulled her close and kissed her. What was happening? She didn't know. This powerful man had her locked in an embrace. She didn't hesitate as he slid his tongue into her mouth. She was beginning a journey to another level of consciousness; a level where time stood still and only she and the Representative existed.

The buttons of her blouse were flying through the air. With the hands of a practiced magician, he unhooked her bra and began touching every inch of her ample breasts. She was hot. Her disbelief in what was happening was drowned out by the thought that this man loved her, wanted her and wouldn't stop until he was satisfied. He was so powerful. What could she do? She surrendered.

He was working her backside up onto the dining table while her pants were coming off. He tore her panties and began licking her. She watched in amazement as this man of power held his face between her legs. Her excitement heightened to a level she never knew existed.

He was undressing quickly. He led her head to his member. It looked huge. It looked delectable. She kissed, sucked and licked this representative of her Representative until it was harder and stronger.

She was on the table again. He entered her. Just the feeling of him entering her almost brought her to orgasm. Then she was lost in the rhythmic motion as he took her again and again, higher and higher, deeper and deeper, more powerful and stronger than she had ever felt before in her life. She felt a pulsing within her. It was too much. She experienced the strongest and longest orgasm ever.

When she returned to a more conscious state, Representative Lewis was lying on top of her breathing heavily with a look that she thought was what ecstasy would look like.

After some time, he got up off the table. Their combined sweat squished as he slid off of her glistening body. She lied there on the table trying to relive their experience. She thought it was over. She heard him in the bathroom rummaging around. She smiled.

He reappeared with her K-Y jelly in his hand. He held out his hand. Without a thought, she extended her hand into his. He led her the three steps to the arm of the sofa bed and leaned her over it. She heard a lathering sound behind her. His hand was searching her backside until it found her anus. She didn't hesitate as he slid his member into it. She pushed. He pushed. She was rising in excitement again.

"Hello."

What? "Hello."

"Cheryl?"

"Oh Cliff, yes, it's Cheryl."

"How did you reach me here?"

"I spoke with Barb; she'd said that you had to stop by your office tonight. I just kept trying."

"Yeah I did. But you're still lucky that you caught me because I only stopped for some reports that I left. I'm tired and I'm on my way home."

"I know it's late but I just had to talk with you."

"What's up?"

"I lost my job today."

"What?"

"Yeah, next Friday's my last day. Bob found out that I had completed my school requirements and he said that meant that I couldn't continue in the intern program any more."

"But you haven't graduated yet."

"I know. I told him that, but he said it didn't matter if the ceremony was outstanding, that technically, I had graduated. Then he called around and got a couple of people to agree with him."

"Well, I'm not sure what to say."

"Can you help me find something? If I have to go back to Howells, I might as well disappear from the face of the earth."

"I'm sure it's not that bad."

"When was the last time you were in Howells?"

"I visit there regularly to speak with my constituents. And it looks as if I may be visiting it with greater regularity."

"Don't even say that."

"I'm just kidding. Let me make some calls and see what I can do. Now get some sleep. I'll talk to you soon."

"Ooh, I love you."

"I love you too. Good night, Cheryl."

"Good night, Cliff."

9 days earlier

Cheryl Chapin entered the doors to the Department of the Interstate Commerce Commission as she would do for only seven more times. It still seemed so strange. How could this be happening? What sinister elements had ruined her plans for continued ecstasy with Cliff? How was she going to be with him in Howells? This couldn't happen!

Her heart was beginning to pound from fear.

No! Cliff was going to find her a job. She would stay in Washington forever. It will be better than being an intern.

"Cheryl."

"Maria, good morning."

"I hope it is. How are you doing?"

"I'm OK. It'll be fine."

"So, you talked to … him."

"Yes. He's going to make some calls. I'm sure that something will open up for me."

"Good. I hope so. Let's get some coffee."

Bob was as pompous as ever. Making sure that Cheryl arrived on time and worked her shift. What does he think? He's such a loser. He thinks everyone is a slacker. The minutes ticked by as Cheryl fanned the flames of hope that somehow Cliff was making progress. Her future was in his hands now. She could only wait. Not patiently, but she waited.

Finally, she was set free and she ran to her house and called Cliff's office. "Representative Lewis' Office, how may I direct your call?"

"Is the Representative in?"

"No, he's not."

"Barbara Gomez, please."

"Please hold while I transfer the call."

"This is Barbara Gomez, how may I help you?"

"Barb? It's Cheryl. I need to talk to Cliff."

"That's going to be tough. He's been in the Armed Services Committee meeting all afternoon and it doesn't look like it's going to end soon. They've ordered dinner in."

"Shit! Did he tell you what happened?"

"We didn't get a chance to talk beyond 'hello' and 'goodbye'. He had the Budget Oversight Committee meeting this morning and he dropped some reports, picked up some others and he was out of here. Like I said, I haven't seen him since."

"Well, I'm out on the street. Bob found out that I completed my requirements to graduate and next Friday is my last day at ICC."

"Whoa, run that by me again. You don't even have to graduate anymore to become ineligible?"

"Apparently not. Anyway, Cliff said that he would make some calls for me and try to find me something permanent."

"Well, honey, I don't think you're going to find out anything today. Give him some time. Call me in a couple of days."

"A couple of days? Barb, I've got less than two weeks. If I don't find something, I'm dead. I'll be back in Howells making compost heaps for my Dad's farm."

Barb, laughing, "Please, Cheryl. You're too funny. It'll be all right. I'll check with Cliff tomorrow and see what he's found."

"Thanks, you're an angel."

"You're my girl."

"Yeah, I'm your girl."

Cheryl didn't feel like anyone's girl. She felt alone. She couldn't keep focused on anything. She tried to read. She tried to watch TV. It was useless. She was useless. She was feeling insignificant. This useless, disposable intern. Who would miss her when she left? Hopefully, Cliff would. But he didn't seem like it today. He was too busy playing the role of Representative. And, meanwhile, she would just disappear from the scene and after a year or two even Cliff's memory of her would fade. Oh, God! A fate worse than death. Insignificance!

Shit. What was she going to do? What if Cliff couldn't find her a job? She'd better think about that and come up with a plan or she'll lose Cliff forever. What could she do? Well, she doesn't have to stay in Howells. She could move to Phoenix. She'll get a job and a place of her own. That way, she can see Cliff every time he flies into and out of the State. She can join his re-election committee and spend all of her spare time working for him.

That's it.

And then when he's re-elected he can say goodbye to that overbearing bitch, Pat, and he'll be all hers.

But, it would be better to stay in Washington.

But, she could live in Phoenix.

Still, she wanted to stay here.

Somewhere between those two thoughts, Cheryl fell asleep.

8 day earlier

A little more tired than usual, Cheryl Chapin entered the doors to the Department of the Interstate Commerce Commission as she would do for only six more times. Still, she was playing over and over again all the different scenarios that might occur, trembling at some of the possibilities and rejoicing in others. She was nearly at the door of her department when she realized that there was no Maria. No one to wake her from her nightmare, to bring her into the reality of today. No one to offer her coffee.

She went looking. "Maria."

"Hi, muñeca."

"You're here already? What are you looking for … brownie points from Bob?"

"Yeah, I wish they were worth something. No, I got more assignments from Bob yesterday. It's going to take me some extra time this week to finish everything."

"What are you working on? Maybe I can help."

"It's some consolidation of crude oil and gasoline movements across state lines over the last four months. Bob thinks he can get his two cents in on the Saudi Arabia thing. As if gasoline movements have anything to do with the Saudis cutting our fuel off."

"Hey, that's what I was working on."

"Maybe Bob caught you sleeping yesterday, too."

"That man is such a loser. I'm glad I'm leaving soon."

"You go, girl."

Talk about gone and forgotten, Cheryl had already been replaced. And it hadn't even been a week! Now what? Even that little distraction called 'work' was taken from her. All she had left to do was think and worry. So, she thought and worried all morning.

As she was leaving for lunch, she caught up with Maria. "Maria."

"What's up?"

"Since Bob's got you doing my work for me, I'm going to be late from lunch. Cover for me will you?"

"No hay problema. I'll tell Bob that you're in the Ladies Room with your monthly visit. He won't ask twice."

"Thanks, Hon."

Cheryl went directly to the Office of Representative Cliff Lewis.

"Good afternoon."

"Good afternoon, I'd like to see Barbara Gomez, please."

"Just a moment. Please take a seat."

A few minutes later, Barb came out with her pad and pen in hand. "Cheryl, I thought it was some one important. Phyllis told me a young applicant was here to see me."

"She was right; but we've had that conversation before. Barb, I need to talk with Cliff."

"Cheryl, I don't know what to tell you. He's been in the Armed Services Committee meeting all morning and it looks like he'll be there all afternoon. You know, we're trying to broker the peace between Saudi Arabia and Israel. But every time we talk to the Saudis and have a concession for Israel, the Israelis already know what's coming and we get blown out of the water. They think there's an Israeli mole working here—very high up."

"Isn't there always a mole? What does this have to do with Cliff?"

"It's his committee that is working to ferret out the mole. There's only twenty-two people on the AS Committee, and since this started, each Rep. only gets to bring in one staffer. They tightened things down, but the information keeps flying out of here. And it's highly confidential … and it's new. Who's ever tied in is tied in tight."

"Fucking Israelites, fucking Saudis, fucking moles, I don't want to hear any of this. All I want is to talk to Cliff."

"Well, you're looking for an Act of Congress, and remember, Congress doesn't act."

Cheryl snuck back into her department and was back in her cubicle before anyone noticed her. She pretended to work on the figures that Bob was looking for by next week to single-handedly resolve the Saudi issue.

But she knew that Maria was doing the real numbers, the ones that Bob would use next week.

The day ended and Cheryl left without a sound. She went home and had a light dinner. What now? Was she going to sit around the apartment and work through the same scenarios ad nauseum?

No. She was going to see Cliff, no matter what the cost.

She took a taxi to the Capitol and walked to his apartment. It was quite a misnomer to call her little place and his grand home the same name of 'apartment'. She had been in his place only twice. He didn't like to have his neighbors become familiar with her. Like all Washingtonians, they loved to gossip. And when his wife came to town, she stayed there too. It just wouldn't be good to have them telling Pat about guests by name. Cheryl understood.

But tonight was different. She had to see him. She had to talk to him. She had to wait for him.

It started to rain, lightly at first. Cheryl began thinking about going back home. She never liked her home, for as long as she can remember. It wasn't anything … or anybody. It was everything … everybody. All through grade school, she was the tall girl in the back row of all of the class pictures. Always the one who stood out, always hunching over to blend in with the crowd but never succeeding. It was Dad always calling her 'my ugly duckling' who promised that she would become a beautiful swan one day. She was the girl who grew boobs first. Another reason for the boys to heckle her. But, if it wasn't for her boobs, she wouldn't have had many dates. They just wanted to touch them. She kept telling herself that she didn't care. But the whole time she hated her home, her little town, having to be groped to see a movie. She had to get out. And get out she did. First, was a ticket to Tempe and Arizona State University. She blew out the air of her small town and breathed in a breath of fresh air. It was a breath of big air. It didn't leave any room for any of the old baggage that she brought with her.

After sophomore year, she had the opportunity to try for one of the intern positions open to Arizona residents. It was during the discovery and interview process that she met Barbara Gomez. She had contacted the Office of her local Representative, Cliff Lewis, and was directed to Barb. Barb was so nice to her and she really wanted to get Cheryl the position. She said it would be good for Representative Lewis to show his constituents that he is working for them in every arena.

And it was here in Washington, D.C. where the beautiful swan appeared. And it was Cliff who did it. He made her feel beautiful. He made her feel wanted. He made her feel important.

And here she was, standing in the pouring rain, faced with the possibility that the beautiful swan would die and she would go back to being the ugly duckling. Every cell in her body sighed.

She saw Cliff. She ran across the street to meet him as he walked towards the door of his apartment.

"Cheryl?! What are you doing here? Look at you, you're soaked. Come on, let's get inside."

Without a thought, she let his strong left hand cradle her right arm and they walked silently into his luxurious home.

Once inside the door, Cliff said, "Let me take off your coat. There; now go into the bathroom and take off those clothes and go dry yourself."

"Cliff," she grabbed at his lapels, "tell me you got me a job. I can't go back to Howells. Tell me."

"I'll tell you, but first, go dry off. And put on some of my clothes. I'll fix us a drink."

Cheryl flew into the bathroom. He did it! He saved her! She knew he would, she knew it. Every cell of her body came back to life. She threw her clothes everywhere and dried herself with his white, terrycloth towel. She danced into the adjoining bedroom to find some clothes that fit.

Cliff was bringing two bourbon and sodas to the sofa when Cheryl entered from the bedroom. She was wearing one of his ties.

"It was the only thing that fit."

"Cheryl. Here, let me help you."

Cliff walked toward her and grabbed the tie as he continued through the doorway into the bedroom. They didn't make it past the bed.

Cheryl rolled over; sweat dripping off her glistening body. "I need to dry off again."

"More than that, we need a shower. Let's go."

"Wait, tell me. Tell me everything."

"Tell you what?"

"Tell me what you found for me."

Cliff hesitated. "I haven't found anything, yet."

"You said …"

"What? You're standing in the doorway, soaking wet, catching a cold and I told you to dry off and we'd talk. We're talking."

"You said you'd tell me."

"I told you…. look, I've been in committee for two days. I haven't had a minute to myself. I'll do what I can, but you knew this day was coming."

"You don't understand." Cheryl said getting up from the bed. Cliff rolled over and tried to grab her hand.

"Don't touch me." Cheryl stormed into the bathroom. What was she going to do now? Her best hope for salvation was in bed lying to her. Letting her give her body and soul like she had never given him before and the whole time he knew he was lying. He hadn't done anything.

She put on her still wet clothes that had now become colder than before. She threw off his tie. It landed in the toilet. "Too bad." She walked down the hallway that led to the Living Room. Cliff was there in a robe.

"Cheryl." He walked toward her

"You don't understand" she stiff-armed him and went directly to the front door. She grabbed her still wet coat and walked outside.

7 days earlier

Despite herself, Cheryl Chapin entered the doors to the Department of the Interstate Commerce Commission as she would do for only five more times. She was still furious. Although she had tossed and turned all night, she was too angry to be tired. Her thoughts carried her to the door of her department. Again, no Maria. Her life had changed forever. She thought that she'd better get on with it.

She made her way to her cubicle without encountering anyone. Instead of pretending to work, she went to work for herself. She began surfing through websites of all of the government agencies, looking for any opening that she could turn into an opportunity. After hours of searching she finally found something in the State Department. It wasn't much, a translator position, but she knew Hebrew from the time she was born and the job was right here in Washington.

Without asking for cover, Cheryl extended her lunch break again and strode over to the State Department building. She found her way to the Human Resources Department, filled out an application and waited while they copied her current U.S. Government ID badge. She felt better. Finally, her life was in her hands. To hell with Bob, to hell with Cliff; she'd show them.

She scurried back to her desk and continued her search. The rest of the afternoon was fruitless, but she was still riding the wave of accomplishment at applying for the job at State. Cheryl went home, prepared herself a snack of cheese and fruit and bread and put it in the refrigerator. She quickly changed into her running clothes and jogged out to Franklin Park, just a few miles from her apartment. Now that life was worth living again, it was worth jogging again.

She loved to jog. It started out as an excuse to get out of the house, to be alone without being closed in by four walls. But over time, she began exercising her mind as much as she was exercising her body. She would bring her problems with her and with each forward stroke of her feet, she would imagine the chain of events that would occur if she did this. And then she would follow the consequences of doing that. She would play out life for weeks or months in advance until she was satisfied which choice would be the best for her.

Now that she was going to be staying in Washington, she needed to decide what to do about Cliff. He turned out to be like every other man; he just wanted to feel her boobs. But she couldn't bring herself to believe that. Cliff loved her. She knew that. He didn't mean to hurt her, men are just insensitive. They have this over-inflated sense of self worth. 'Wait here Cheryl, while I go save the fucking world.' It isn't their fault. Too much testosterone. That was certainly Cliff's problem. He's an animal. He's voracious. And God, she loved him so much.

Another successful run.

She would take him back.

She jogged home. Took off her sweaty clothes and couldn't help thinking of the night before when she had thrown her wet clothes around Cliff's bathroom. She began flinging her clothes around her tiny room. Last night, they flew through the air and landed on the ground. Tonight, every one was slapping against the wall and flopping to the floor. She walked naked to the shower and bathed. She dried and put on her socks, sweat pants and an ASU football jersey top. Even though it was Spring, the nights were still cold.

She poured herself a glass of chardonnay and took her dinner plate from the refrigerator.

She was just finishing her glass of wine when there was a knock at her door. She looked out the small window next to the door. It was Cliff. He did love her. She'd take him back, but she wasn't going to boff him tonight.

She opened the door. Cliff flashed a smile and walked into her little place. "Cheryl, I'm sorry."

"I'm sorry, too. It's all my fault."

"No, I know that this is important to you."

"No, really, I didn't give you a chance to talk. It's just that…. forget it." Cheryl fell on him with her arms falling around his neck. Cliff kissed her softly on the cheek and whispered in her ear, "I made a few calls and there may be something in the Justice Department."

"Oooh." Cheryl jumped up and down.

"Maybe. I don't have any promises"

"I know. I'm just happy that you took the time to help me. And, I want you to know, that I put in an application with State for a translator job"

"Very good"

Cheryl jumped up and forward and landed in Cliff's arms again. They kissed. And then … they kissed. Cheryl was wrapping her entire being around Cliff.

The next thing she knew, they were lying naked on the floor; both of their bodies glistening with sweat. She looked over at Cliff to see his face in an expression that she had learned was the look that ecstasy used when it was satiated.

She turned her head and fell asleep.

6 days earlier

Weary but happy, Cheryl Chapin entered the doors to the Department of the Interstate Commerce Commission as she would do for only four more times. She settled into her desk immediately and called Cliff's Office.

"Representative Lewis' Office, how may I direct your call?"

"Barbara Gomez, please."

"Please hold while I transfer the call."

"This is Barbara Gomez, how may I help you?"

"Barb? It's Cheryl. Is Cliff in the office?"

"The Representative *is* in, please hold while I transfer the call."

"Hello?"

"Hi Cliff, it's me."

"Just a minute." After a short pause, "Cheryl"

"Cliff, I just wanted to call to thank you for coming by last night. It meant a lot to me."

"I know."

"How did you get out of the AS meeting today?"

"Oh, they've set some sort of trap to try and catch the mole. We're 'on hold' until they come up with something. Look, I'm going to be tied up for a while. Pat is flying in this afternoon and she'll be here all week."

"Well, shit, I was glad that you were out of the AS meetings and now I get hit with the wicked witch of the West."

"Cheryl, please."

"Well, what about the Justice job? How am I going to know what's going on if you're out of commission? When am I going to see you next? I have to see you again."

"As soon as I hear anything on the Justice job, I'll have my office send an e-mail to your ICC address. And, believe me, if there's any chance that I can get away, I'll send word. It may just be a date and time, but you'll be there for me, won't you?"

"Oh, I'll be there alright, wearing your tie."

"Please don't remind me about the tie."

"I am sorry about that."

"You can make it up to me. I gotta go."

"I love you."
"Bye."

God, she loved that man. But, God, she hated that woman. Why does he stay with her? She's so phony with that short, blond, bouncy hair of hers. She looks like she just walked out of a Pert commercial. All the time. She had actually met Pat once. It was freaky. Why in the world would this woman strike up a conversation with an intern? She was pretty good at spousal avoidance at the parties that they attended, but this one time Pat blind-sided her. The next thing she knows, Pat's introducing herself and going through Cliff's credentials like she's reading the ingredients of a ketchup bottle. It was 'I gotta get a drink' and she was out of there. Obviously, the woman's a frigid bitch.

She had to stop thinking about it. It was only going to lead to the inevitable, 'men are the stupidest species on the face of the earth'. And, last she checked, Cliff was a man.

But thoughts of Cliff and, to a lesser extent, Pat filled her head until her work day, and her work week, were finally over.

At home, the thought of putting her life 'on hold' for two days was depressing. She drank the rest of her Chardonnay and went to bed. Maybe the morning sunshine would put a brighter face on this bleak situation.

5 days earlier

Ugh!

Cheryl woke up to a dark and dreary Saturday morning. 'A perfect fit', she thought. The clouds outside looked ominous and she was a little hung over from too much wine last night. The thought of all the things that couldn't be done to move her life forward depressed her further.

'I have to get out of this house' she thought, but the weather wasn't going to make that easy. 'I know', it dawned on her. 'I'll do some of the things I've just never had time to do, like go to the Smithsonian Institute!'

Cheryl was showered, dressed and gone within 30 minutes. Of course, she started at the Air & Space Museum. Like most people, flight fascinated Cheryl. Not to the point that she ever wanted to study and understand the physics involved. It was fascinating enough just to wonder in awe. And then to see the Mercury and Gemini space modules—they look like models, not something that a full-sized man would climb into of his own free will!

Next, Cheryl went to the Museum of Natural History. The array of fossils and the endless variety of species was mind-boggling. She could have spent a day in that museum alone. But she had promised herself when she first moved to Washington to go the Holocaust Museum. She made her way across Madison Drive and down 14th and found the line for the museum. The day was still dark and cloudy, but the rains had held off so far. An hour later she entered the darkness that lasts 40 minutes but stays with you forever. Outside, Cheryl cried. She cried for the people in the pictures; she cried for their families; she cried for Humanity, that anyone so cold and uncaring for the lives of others could have walked this earth.

When she thought her tears had run out, Cheryl walked. She walked in no direction in particular, she just walked. Slowly, she re-entered this world. She was surrounded by people, walking to their houses, walking to their work and walking to the shops. Revived from her experience, Cheryl realized that she was hungry, it was almost mid-afternoon. She began paying attention to the shops and restaurants as she passed them. She stopped at a few to check the serving times and the menu. She stopped outside the "Quilted Bear" to check their menu hanging in the window. It looked good. She glanced inside to the restaurant tables and ambiance. It looked cozy. And then … Cheryl's eyes became glassy. Her stare was unending. It couldn't be. It couldn't be. This can't be happening. But, it was. There, in the corner booth, out of the way of the public view, out of the way of photographers and alone, sat Cliff with that bitch, Pat. They were laughing, drinking wine; he was holding her hand across the tabletop. Cheryl's thoughts went off like a string of firecrackers; 'What is going on? He told me he's only with her for publicity and social gatherings. What? Does he love her? Look at him; he's holding her hand; he's laughing; he's having the time of his life. What? Does he love her? Does he think he can love me and her? No way. You just go right ahead, you lying prick. Just go ahead; get her drunk and take her back to your bed and fuck her. But, just know this, bitch, he fucked me there first. I fucked him there two days ago; I fucked him dry. He probably hasn't even changed the sheets. You can smell OUR sweat when he fucks you.'

Cheryl stammered as she wandered off in any direction. Her vision blurred as the tears welled in her eyes. But the anger within her burned them off before they could fall to her cheeks. After who knows how many blocks of walking aimlessly, Cheryl felt alone and exposed. She needed shelter, she needed warmth; she needed to go home.

When she closed the door to her apartment behind her, Cheryl cried. But now, all of her tears were for herself. She felt sorry for the girl who was always the tallest in grade school. She felt sorry for the girl with the biggest boobs in middle school. She felt sorry for the "ugly duckling" in high school. And she felt sorry for the beautiful swan that only lived for two years.

Finally, she ran out of tears.

Her blank mind slowly let thoughts enter. 'I need to let Cliff explain. I'm sure there's an explanation. How could it be that he loves her and not me when he gave himself to me two days ago … and innumerable times before?'

Slowly, she picked up her telephone and called Cliff's cell phone.

Ring

Ring

Ring

Ring

Ring

"This is Representative Lewis, please leave a message and I'll return your call."

Cheryl hung up. 'Maybe he's busy. Maybe he's too busy holding her hand to answer the fucking phone.'

Cheryl dialed again.

Ring

Ring

Ring

Ring

Ring

"This is Representative Lewis, please leave a message and I'll return your call."

Cheryl hung up.

He wasn't going to answer. She'll wait. He'll have an answer for her.

Now, she realizes that she's really hungry. The rains have begun and she doesn't have anything other than chips and snacks in the house. Thank God for pizza delivery.

It's hard not to be satisfied after a half pepperoni half Canadian bacon medium pizza and a diet Coke. What a wonderful paradox. A piece of chocolate may have put her in a decent mood. Regardless, it was time to call Cliff again. Cheryl dialed.

Ring

Ring

"This is Cliff."

"Cliff, it's Cheryl."

"I'm getting dressed for dinner; can I call you back, later?"

"Cliff, I saw you and Pat today in the restaurant. I thought the husband-wife thing was for the press and your congressional buddies. I didn't see either of them this afternoon."

"What? You're talking nonsense. I don't have time for this right now."

"I need an explanation."

"Well, I guess I'll have to explain it later, when it makes more sense. Don't call me again. I told you, you can't call me this week."

"Cliff"

"Good bye"

Cheryl was furious. She knew he was dodging her; buying time. Obviously, the bitch wasn't around; otherwise he would have called her Bill and thanked her for the update. Something's up with him.

The more she thought through this line of reasoning the more depressed she became. Her life had become a roller coaster and she was rolling down again … she wanted to raise her arms and scream, but she was drained of all energy. Her head flopped into her hand as desolation rolled over her like the clouds had this afternoon. Tears welled up in her eyes and rolled gently down her cheeks.

4 days earlier

Cheryl's eyes opened. Immediately, there was a sharp pain in the back and right side of her neck. She was sitting on the floor. Right where she was last night.

It all came back to her; the same feelings of anger mixed with disgust mixed with fear, all overlaying her love for Cliff that still resided deep within her being. She tried to move her head but she was without resolve. Her sleep had brought her no energy. She found a direction where the pain was less and stared.

Her eyes were dry when she finally blinked. It felt like her eye lids had Velcro lining as she blinked again and again. She had to move, but she had no energy, no desire.

Cheryl moved her head slowly. The pain rolled from one side to the other, slowly. She stood up. She reeled slightly as a boxer who got up just before the count of ten. Again Cheryl moved her head slowly. The pain was continuous and dull. She slightly stretched her shoulders as she walked to the bureau in the living room. She flipped through her two dozen DVDs and grabbed *Casablanca*. She detoured to a bag of chips before she loaded the DVD, eased onto the sofa and began the mechanical movements of chip-to-face and hand-to-bag.

As always, at the end of the movie, she cried. It never made any sense to her. How could Ilsa leave Rick? How could Rick leave Ilsa and, literally, hand her over to Victor? They were a perfect couple overcome by circumstances; the war, she had married, he was still running away from home.

Then she realized—this was her life. She was like Rick, running away from home. She came to this city and met her Ilsa, the love of her life, her soul-mate. Unfortunately, Cliff had married. And now they were being separated by circumstances. According to the movie, she should just hand Cliff over to Pat and walk away. But she never understood that. She wasn't going to make Rick's mistake. One word from Rick and Ilsa would have been by his side for life. She wasn't going to hand Cliff over to anybody. He was hers … for life.

She looked down at her empty bag. She needed a soda. There had to be some crackers in the drawer.

3 days earlier

Cheryl Chapin entered the doors to the Department of the Interstate Commerce Commission for the last Monday. Now, Maria del Carmen Morales was nowhere to be found for gossip or coffee.

Cheryl weaved her way silently through the maze of cubicles to hers. She waited silently for the staff meeting. She didn't speak, she didn't sip coffee, she didn't think.

Bob opened the staff meeting, "I would like to announce that Cheryl Chapin will be leaving us as of this Friday. To celebrate her new life, we will have cake and ice cream in this room on Friday at 3:00 PM."
"Thanks, Bob. I know it's really a celebration of my departure"
"Not at all. No one is going to miss you more than me."

Bob passed out assignments to everyone except Cheryl. "But please be advised that Cheryl will be available to everyone for any assistance that you need."
"Thanks? Bob?"
"Well Cheryl, I need you to be here working this week. You're still on the payroll."
"Since you put it so sweetly...." Cheryl led the group out of the meeting room.

Once back in cube, Cheryl went right to work. She checked the job listings on-line. Nothing new. She contacted Human Resources regarding her application to the State Department. They are still accepting applications. So, she called Cliff's special message number. He had given it to her and told her that, as long as she was in a secure location, her message would be secure since this was a private message phone that was not accessed by his staff. Therefore, she had no qualms about telling him everything on her mind.
"Cliff; it's Cheryl. I just wanted to leave a message to tell you that I understand that you're doing everything that you can to get me a job and

if it doesn't work out, it's OK. I'm not going to worry about it. We'll find a way to be together, I know it.

And I want you to know that last Thursday was terrific. I didn't mean to spoil it this weekend and I won't do it again. Forgive me? I know you do. I love you! Try to find sometime this week. OK? Bye."

With that she wandered the department looking for things to do to keep her mind off of everything else. She did well at her task and before too long lunch time had arrived. She went alone to the Golden Diner just around the corner and ordered a BLT with fries and a grape soda. She had been to South America with her parents and it was there that she first tried the fruity, carbonated sodas. You don't find them often in the States but they're all over the place in those third world counties. They just love sugar. Well, she got hooked on grape and ordered it first every time. Only about a quarter of the places carry it, so most of the time she has to settle for Coke.

As she ate she kept thinking of other options for a job. It didn't necessarily have to be in government, but it had to pay enough to keep her in her apartment. She remembered that she had some e-mail addresses on her home computer of some people that she had met at some of the dinner parties. Phyllis Taylor was an architect and interior designer; Jenny Cheung worked in an Art Gallery. What the hell, it couldn't hurt to try.

After lunch she stopped by her apartment to pick up the addresses she needed. How strange—the top bolt wasn't locked. Could she have left it unlocked? She's never done that before. The door's locked. She went in and briefly checked around. Nothing is out of place—all's quiet. She turned on the computer and wrote down the addresses for Phyllis and Jenny. When she left, she very conscientiously locked the bolt on the door.

Cheryl arrived at work late. Who cares? She wrote two excellent e-mails, reviewing her work experience, her interest and her availability. She cruised the department looking for things to keep her busy.

Cheryl went home. The door and the bolt were both locked. How freaky. She changed into her running clothes and jogged around Franklin

Park. This time she tried to keep things in perspective. It wasn't what happened, but how she reacted to it. Those words were so easy to say and so hard to follow. It seemed that every time something didn't go her way, her first reaction was anger and violence. This time she had to be better. There were only two things that could occur. She could stay or she could move back to Arizona. Either way, she had a plan. Staying in Washington was simple. Everything would be the same. If she moved back home, she'd look for a job in Phoenix and wouldn't accept anything else. Then she could get her own place and things would be different, but good.

She was feeling better.

Another successful jog.

She jogged home and took off her sweaty clothes. This time she let them fall in a pile at her feet. She stepped out of the pile of clothes and looked carefully at her body in the mirror. She was beginning to like herself more. Her hair was long and curly and black; a direct result of her heritage. Her face was OK. Two eyes, two ears, a nose and a mouth, she thought. She laughed at her joke. Her breasts were huge. She knew it. With large nipples and large areolas. She cradled her breasts in each hand. Then she slid her hands down and into her waist and out at her hips. Her hips were big. She also thought her thighs were massive, but Cliff said he loved them. Whatever.

She stepped into the shower and continued her self-evaluation.

She dried and put on her socks, work out shorts and the same ASU football jersey top that had brought her luck last week.

Now, what to do. There was no one she wanted to call and talk to other than Cliff and she couldn't do that. She didn't want to drink another bottle of wine to drown her sorrows. So, she called for Chinese take out and picked out another movie. Oh yes, '*An Affair to Remember*'. She'll be crying tonight.

It'll do her good to cry over somebody else today.

2 days earlier

Cheryl Chapin entered the doors to the Department of the Interstate Commerce Commission for the last Tuesday.

Her work day seemed to be a repeat of yesterday, without the staff meeting. She checked the job listings on-line. Still nothing new. She contacted Human Resources regarding her application to the State Department. Nada. But today, she controlled herself and didn't call Cliff. She checked her e-mail religiously throughout the day waiting for notification. Nothing came.

As the day wore on, she had come to the belief that she was not destined to stay in Washington. If she had nothing definitive by the end of work tomorrow, she would have to make her plans to fly back home this weekend. Fuck, she hated that option.

But, she had promised to stay positive. It would be alright. She wasn't going to make Rick's mistake. Men are such assholes sometimes.

Cheryl went home, had a light dinner and thought about the steps she would need to take to move home. Obviously, the simple tasks of buying a plane ticket, packing and breaking her lease. All that was simple, but the difficult part begins when she lands in Phoenix. She would give her parents the weekend to paw all over her, but on Monday, she would be in Phoenix, preparing and distributing her résumé. It wouldn't be easy. Her parents think that Howells is the place to live. For them, it probably is. But she was different. She was going to enjoy her life. And that meant being with Cliff.

Cliff.

Still, no word from Cliff. What a bummer. If she was going to have to go home, she had to see him before she left. She hoped that he felt the same way. She hoped that he was finding a way—a time, a place—for them to meet. She slid her hands up the inner thighs of both legs and thought, "If I could just wrap these massive thighs around him one more time before I go." She laughed.

She went to bed and continued with her thoughts of Cliff and imagined that her touch was his.

1 day earlier

Cheryl Chapin entered the doors to the Department of the Interstate Commerce Commission for the last Wednesday.

Today was beyond déjà-vu. She checked the job listings on-line. Still nothing new. She contacted Human Resources regarding her application to the State Department. Less than nada. But today, she couldn't control herself. She called Cliff's message phone. "Cliff, Cheryl. Hey babe, I guess I'm not going to get that Justice job and I haven't heard anything from State although I've followed up everyday. Anyway, I'll be making my arrangements to go back home tomorrow. I've got to leave by the weekend so I can start looking for a job in Phoenix on Monday. I really want to see you before I go. Send me a message. OK? I love you. I miss you."

She checked her e-mail throughout the day waiting for something from Cliff's office, but she had lost her religion. She was checking it so that she could say that she checked it. She didn't expect anything and nothing came.

She went home and changed into her running clothes and jogged around Franklin Park. She jogged but she couldn't think. It was like she was in shock. The reality of the full situation had finally dawned on her; she was going home. She was leaving Cliff behind. In reality, she didn't know when she would see him again. She hadn't heard a word. She was even in too much shock to get angry over it.

She was through jogging.

She jogged home and took off her sweaty clothes. She let them fall in a pile at her feet. She stepped out of the pile of clothes, looked at herself in the mirror. She quickly slid her hands down her sides until she got to her massive thighs. She shook her head in disgust and stepped into the shower.

She dried herself and threw on a robe. She sat with her feet on the sofa and her legs pressed against her breast. She sat stunned. It seemed liked weeks, although it was only two hours later that she broke out of her trance long enough to trudge into bed.

She spent a fitful night trying to sleep. It escaped her.

Today

Cheryl Chapin entered the doors to the Department of the Interstate Commerce Commission for the last Thursday.

Cheryl contacted her landlord and explained the entire story in its every detail, so that he would know that she was an unfortunate soul who needed his sympathy and her deposit back despite the short notice. At least she still had her charm; he gave in even before she ended.

"It sounds like you're going to need your deposit back before the weekend."

"Oh, that would be great. How can I ever thank you?"

"Don't start that. I remember when I was young. I could have used a break here and there."

"Thank you, thank you, thank you."

"OK, OK; I'll try to stop by your apartment by Friday."

"I'll see you then and thanks again."

Next she got on-line and began her search for a flight. Of course, at this late date every airline was going to rip her a new asshole for a ticket. "Rip her a new asshole". After two years with Cliff, she understood why that expression was started. It certainly could be painful at times. She smiled to herself. Well, at least she was getting her deposit back; that will help. She made her arrangements.

Finally, she called Cliff on his message number. "Cliff, it's lonely Cheryl. I have a flight to Phoenix on Saturday. I leave at 11:05 AM. That leaves us about 30 hours to get together. I swear, I think I'll bust if I don't see you. So, help a girl out, OK? I love you."

Cheryl left work early and went home to begin packing. After she was left with just the things that she would need over the next day and a half, she called her mom to give her the flight information.

"Honey, that's great! I mean, it's sad that it had to happen like this, but I am so excited. I can't wait. We'll both be at the airport to pick you up.

Oh, this is great! I'm canceling everything that I was doing this weekend. I don't even know what it is, but it's cancelled."

"OK, mom, I'll see you then."

"OK, Cheryl, don't worry about a thing. We'll see you Saturday."

"Yeah, see you Saturday."

Cheryl hung up the phone. She looked around her apartment almost in disbelief. The day after tomorrow she would be gone—back home with her parents in Howells. It was almost surreal. Last week she was working as an intern and making love to the man she loved and this week she's on her way back home. Cliff. What was she going to do without seeing Cliff everyday? Would she really get a job in Phoenix? How was she going to make love to Cliff while she was living with her parents? Cliff said it would be alright. They'd find a way to be together when he came back to visit with his constituents—which he promised to do more often than he had been over the past two years.

She sat on her overstuffed chair and looked carefully at her efficiency apartment. A kitchen with a dining table, a bathroom and the sofa that pops out into a bed. She remembers the first time she and Cliff made love on the bed. He stopped by after one of the many State Dinners he attended. He smelled like liquor but he was so powerful, so focused, focused on her. It all happened so quickly. He was in her door and before she knew it, he was in her mouth. He was an animal. Nothing else existed except him. She was hot. He was bigger than she had ever expected. It was amazing. They never did open the bed that night. He made love to every orifice of her body.

How many times had they made love since then? It seemed like a thousand but she'd only been here for less than two years, so how could it be? Whatever it was, it wasn't enough. She wanted to see him before she left. He said he couldn't. His wife was in Washington all week. But he said he'd send word if he could get away.

There was a knock at her door. She was startled. Could it be Cliff? She looked out the small window next to the door. No, it's not. It's some guy in a uniform. Maybe he's sending word.

She opened the door with the security latch on. "Cheryl Chapin?" the uniformed man asked.

"Yes, I'm Cheryl."

"I have a message from Representative Lewis. May I come in?"

Oh my God, I am going to see him before I leave, she thought.

"Yes. Yes, please come in."

Cheryl closed the door and unlocked the security lock. She opened up the door. The uniformed man was standing completely still. Like he was guarding the Tomb of the Unknown Soldier or, maybe, completely bored. I guess he doesn't know how exciting this is, she thought.

He came in and closed the door behind him, softly.

She was flustered. Too excited to just stand there.

"Can I get you something to drink?" she asked.

"Ma'am." He said with a nod.

Cheryl turned towards the kitchen on the right. She saw a big hand moving in front of her face. It grabbed her chin. She heard a crack.

The Perpetrator

Friday

Flight 857 from Phoenix Sky Harbor Airport to Reagan International Airport in Washington D.C. is scheduled to leave at 9:05 AM Mountain Time and arrive at 3:37 PM Eastern Time. The first class cabin is light on passengers as Pat looks around before admitting that there is no one interesting to talk to on this flight. By interesting, Pat means political.

Patricia Arlene Lewis nee Teasdale has always been a political animal. She tried for as long as she could remember to be in the political arena. She ran for Student President in high school her Junior and Senior years and had to settle for Secretary and Treasurer, respectively. Finally, in College she became the president of her sorority. It was then, in the throes of that victory, that Pat realized why she had won. There was no man running against her. The unseemly realities of politics reached in and grabbed her by the throat. It was a feeling of helplessness that she will never forget. Oh sure, there have been women elected to offices before and there will be afterwards. But not someone like her. She has blond hair. The first liability. She had been a cheerleader and a volleyball player. The second liability. She was cute. Pat straightened the legs of her pants suit. Even after all these years, she was still athletic and still had the same cute figure that she had during High School and College. Some men still thought of her as pretty. She thought she was too. But that was the last and most deadly liability. The voters, whether in High School or in the State of Arizona, never took her seriously.

People who knew her took her seriously. She should have been born a man. Certainly, there were times when she used her feminine charm and a helpless attitude to get what she wanted, but she was just as comfortable grabbing someone by the short hairs and pulling hard until they relented to her demands.

It was during her reign as sorority president that she met a handsome Political Science major named Clifford Wayne Lewis. Cliff fell in love with her and wooed her without end. He was constantly sending her love notes addressed to P. A. T.

Cliff had an interest in politics and he was extremely charming. A natural, really; except he had no idea how to utilize the tools that God had given him. He was smart enough but he just wasn't motivated. She could lead him to victory.

After graduation, she became his campaign manager for a seat in the State House of Representatives. She was tireless. Meeting and greeting every important member in the party as well as the opposition party. As she expected, when it was time for them to work hard on campaigning, Cliff wanted to play. She kept him on target. Cliff won his first election.

They were married. A political coup. For all the voters who didn't vote for Cliff because they thought he might be too young and irresponsible, he became responsible and serious about the issues overnight with their marriage.

They spent hours discussing the issues faced by the House. He brought home briefs and analyses. Pat devoured all the information and, on occasion, sent him back to bring more reports from his staff. She built a strategy and approach to each issue and trained Cliff on the discussions that needed to occur, with whom and when. He was a quick study and took direction well. They made an excellent team during his tenure as Representative.

After two terms, it was time to move on to State Senator. Certainly, his youth brought in the young vote. His charm had a lock on the older women's vote and Pat, by his side as he spoke strongly on the issues, most of those speeches which she wrote, calmed the large conservative vote that brought Cliff a victory in his first run for Senator. His Senatorship was just as successful, and run the same way. She stayed close to his side and prepped him on the issues and his votes. She attended almost all of the official functions and earned the respect of Cliff's colleagues. She'd heard that they called her PAL, after her initials but also because no one dared make an enemy of her.

It was during his re-election campaign that Pat caught Cliff in the bed of a pick-up truck fucking some young campaign worker. It was an ugly scene. Pat had threatened to divorce Cliff; to ruin his political career; to leave him with nothing. He cried, he begged her to stay; he promised his fidelity. She thought she had him right where she wanted him—under control. After all, she would never divorce him and end her own political career, just when it was starting to get interesting. He behaved himself for a while, but during his second Senate term, she heard rumors of some office groupie who delivered refreshments and gave blow jobs to Senators "in conference".

Then came the Big Leagues. Senator Goldberg had finally retired as U.S. Representative of the 1st District, which included their home town of Prescott. Although the 1st didn't seem to be a friend of Cliff's party, if he ran, it would be against a "rookie". And by now, Pat was no rookie. Pat decided to run, that is, Pat decided that Cliff would run. She called in all of the many favors that she had earned over the years as Representative and Senator and got "the machine" out in full force to elect Cliff. It was a crushing victory and Cliff was humble yet confident as he gave his acceptance speech on Election night.

The Lewis' went to Washington. Everything was completely different inside the beltway. She practically taped Cliff's mouth shut during the first few weeks so that she could get a lay of the land before committing to anything. Everyone saw a friendship with a freshman Representative as an opportunity to increase their voting power by 100%. Everyone was willing to take Cliff under their wing and show him the ropes. With her "gag order" tightly in place, she maneuvered through the maze that is federal politics staying well under the radar screen of the political lions who ruled this jungle. After all, she was a wife; she didn't have a vote. But she had ears. And so many Representatives, Senators, secretaries and aides were willing to explain everything in great detail to the cute, dumb blond. After not too long, she was making progress. He needed to co-sponsor this bill; vote against that amendment and speak to this Committee Chairman about supporting his "crime bill" over lunch. Cliff seemed almost out of his league. He was hanging on by a thread. But he was smart enough to do everything Pat told him to do, when she told him to do it.

Then some of the lions caught on to her game. She decided to back–off. She was put on the distribution list of every report that went to Representative Lewis and she moved back to Prescott and set up "base camp" there. She stayed in contact with Cliff on a daily basis, and many times more than daily. Cliff set up a private message phone number that was not accessible by his staff. Pat would leave detailed instructions for Cliff on upcoming issues if he was tied up in Committee. Cliff would take the instructions and call for clarification of any details that remained fuzzy. He made more trips back to Arizona to be with his constituents than when Pat lived in Washington. By the end of his first term, he had seats on the Budget Committee and the Armed Services Committee. As long as the party held their seats in the next election, his sophomore term looked very promising.

At times she had nightmares that she was really only another "staffer" who researched issues for the Representative and offered conclusions. But then she calmed herself in the knowledge that Cliff didn't make decisions, she did. And he never complained. He never asked to be in charge—to make the decisions. Cliff was Cliff, other things motivated him. Like the stewardess on the flight that Cliff regularly took back and forth to Phoenix. Apparently, he got tired of banging her in the airplane lavatory and they started using a room at the Airport Hilton. That's when some of her friends advised her of the reason for the "flight delays" and the "traffic back-ups". Again she attacked him with both barrels, trying to intimidate him into submission. But, by now, even Cliff knew that she would never divorce him. He was untouchable and he knew it. She was furious. She would get him; maybe not now, but she would get him good. The girl?

The girl went away. Pat read in the paper that the poor, unfortunate soul was raped at knifepoint and disfigured when she resisted. She quit her job shortly thereafter.

That's when Pat stepped up her clandestine activities. She made friends with a couple of computer wiz kids at ASU. They taught her about "administrative access". Every electronic device has an option available, a "back door", for the administrator to read, write, monitor the functions or modify the settings of the device. She gave them the information about Cliff's phone message machine and in less than an afternoon, she had administrative access to the message machine. She could listen to all messages left without Cliff knowing that they had been listened to. She could monitor when Cliff listened to a message and what phone number he called from for the message. She would know if he gave this number out to others to leave him personal messages! And she could track the phone number that was used to leave the message to identify to whom he gave the number.

She bought Cliff a wristwatch; a beautiful Rolex with a gold and silver wrist band. She had a transmitter inserted into it that would receive sound, amplify it and transmit it at 750 megacycles to a range of two miles. She used the watch as a timer and set transmission from 8:00 AM until 7:00 PM, Monday through Friday. Cliff loved the watch and Pat was sure to insist that it become a part of his "image". It did.

On her next trip to Washington, Pat rented an upstairs flat in the Capitol District. She paid cash and set up continued payments in cash through the secretary of the Junior Senator from Nebraska. A fine, young girl who Pat had the opportunity to meet at one of the many dinners around D.C. She immediately fell in love with Karen's honesty and gullibility. So, every month, Karen would dip into the cash that Pat had left for her and stop by the apartment landlord to pay the rent.

Although Pat had told Karen it was a "pie de terre" so she could be alone with Cliff, Pat set up a receiving station for Cliff's wristwatch that recorded transmissions on 1500 feet of reel at a 10X compression. She could get about two weeks of usable information on each tape. Certainly not good enough for CIA surveillance; but adequate for her needs. Each visit to D.C. included some "alone time" when she could review the transmissions and prepare the new tape for receipt of data. Depending on her schedule and Cliff's, she would start the tape immediately or begin operations on her drive to the airport. It was convenient that there seemed to be some State Dinner or Congressional function that she wanted to attend about every two weeks. Sure, she varied it from time to time, sometimes waiting three or four weeks and she usually only stayed a day or two.

Through the message machine, Pat was able to stay on top of Cliff's girlfriends. She laughed to herself; the look on his face every time she named names. And shortly thereafter the girlfriend would stop leaving messages. But Pat wasn't getting much information from the watch transmissions. She was able to critique Cliff's style of discussions with his colleagues and offer suggestions—again, poor Cliff had no idea what brought about the suggestions. But most of it was lame discussions about overinflated spending bills and covert troop movements throughout the globe.

But then came messages from some piece of trash named Cheryl. Once again, Pat confronted Cliff and got the 'deer in the headlights' look. She thought that that would be it. But the messages kept coming. After two or three times of discussing Cheryl, it dawned on Pat that Cliff didn't care that she knew and wasn't going to send this piece of trash on her way.

It was during this time that Israel and Saudi Arabia came to blows. The U. S. jumped in between our most cherished friend and our most important trade partner to keep peace and trade intact. But, as is the case with most friendships, one partner is more committed to the friendship than the other. Israel stopped viewing the United States as a friend and took their 'Israel against the world' stance. The next thing anyone knew, Israel had intelligence secrets of the U.S. Government that hadn't even been shared with the Joint Chiefs. The search for the 'mole' began.

Call it Providence, call it Luck or call it the blessing of the gods, but these events offered before Pat at this time brought her to a conclusion that bordered on the genius. She found the mole; it was that piece of trash named Cheryl. And she'd plant the information to prove it. Oh my God, this is too good. This is like having a royal flush. You know that you're going to win; now, you have to play it to win big. So, Pat could use those useless watch transmissions of the Armed Services Committee meetings, re-write them to small cassette tapes and plant them in Cheryl's apartment for them to be found. She'll have to collect incriminating evidence to put the AS Committee on Cheryl's trail. And, she'll have to give it to the Chairman so Cliff doesn't hear about it. The better the evidence, the faster they'll get to her apartment and the better chance that Cliff won't get wind of anything. At least not yet. Once the girl is killed and dumped, she'll leak Cliff's affair to the 'missing' intern. The press coverage will be invaluable. He'll have the 'plausible deniability' about anything that happened to her. He'll never be a suspect and, eventually, he'll be completely exonerated. The case will fall out of the press and within a year or two every trace of the case will be as forgotten as the file in the 'unsolved cases' cabinet. Then she'll let Cliff know, without telling him, that he'd better not fuck around again. Wow, a home run in anyone's park!

Pat had contacted her wiz kids and got access to the membership files of a few radical Israeli groups and added Cheryl's name to the membership roles during her early college years. Her new best friends got her access to airline records and she added Cheryl to the passenger lists on certain flights to Jerusalem during congressional breaks.

Now, she was heading to Washington to make her move. She didn't dare wait too long; God forbid they find the real 'mole' before she plays her cards! She should get some good, recent information from the watch transmissions since she knew that Cliff has been in conference for the past couple of days. Cliff said that they were setting a trap; he didn't know what it was but she was going to trip it. Tuesday night was a Congressional Dinner with Chairman Russell. She would provide him the evidence that he needed to investigate Cheryl, they would find the tapes in her apartment and Black Ops would be called in to terminate the 'mole'.

"The captain has turned on the 'fasten seatbelt' sign in anticipation of our on-time arrival into Reagan International Airport. Please check that your seat back is in its upright and locked position and that your seat belt is fastened. One of the uniformed flight attendants will be going through the aisle to collect any trash that you may have."

"I'll have some trash for you in about a week." Pat thought to herself.

As always, it took 30 minutes to get her luggage and get out of the airport. Pat went to her flat. In less than an hour she had selected and re-written portions of the Armed Services Committee meetings from last Tuesday afternoon and Wednesday onto three mini cassette tapes. Wednesday was particularly sweet; a new strategy outlined by the Committee. That would make Chairman Russell shift in his seat. She slid the tapes into the zipper portion of her purse, zipped it up and went to the Lewis apartment.

When she arrived at almost six, Cliff was already there.

"Well, you're in early", she said as upbeat as possible.

"I came home early to welcome you. Where have you been?"

"Oh, flight delays, heavy traffic, you know."

What a look on his face, she thought. That was a low blow, even for her. 'But, look at him' she thought, 'he thinks I'm having an affair. Good.'

"Have you had dinner?" he asked sheepishly. "I thought we could get some good Italian."

"No, I haven't eaten, but I'd rather eat in. I'm a little tired so I may turn in early."

They agreed on Thai take-out. Cliff ran out to pick it up and Pat went into the bathroom to shower. She stopped to look at herself in the mirror. Short, blond hair with a natural flip; her eyes were still a deep blue and she had a clear complexion. She smiled. And a cute smile, she thought. What was it that Cliff fell in love with and then fell out of love with? Or did she lose something during the years? She slid her blouse off her shoulders and down her back. She put her hands behind her back and unhooked her bra. It fell on the countertop revealing still perky little breasts that pointed out to the mirror with their little nipples and little areolas. She was 44 years old and still had the strong upper body she had at eighteen. She took off her pants and underpants in one swoop to the floor. She admired her thin hips with the blond patch of hair in the middle. Her thighs were strong; a little large for her taste, but strong thighs had to be larger. She turned sideways and viewed her profile. Her lower stomach was protruding out; but just a little, and not enough to turn Cliff off. What was it? What had she lost? Certainly not anything physical. She walked naked to the shower. If it wasn't physical, then it must be that she had matured and Cliff hadn't. There was nothing she could do about that; she wasn't going to go back to cheerleading. She was in the game.

Dinner came and went with little conversation. As she warned, Pat climbed into bed early and left Cliff to amuse himself alone.

Saturday

Pat woke up around 4:00 AM; her internal clock was still on Mountain Time. She got up and busied herself with unpacking and household chores until Cliff awoke at 6:00 AM. They shared a light breakfast of eggs and toast. Cliff went off to his office for the morning, promising to return for lunch.

That was plenty of time for Pat to do the things that she'd been waiting to do since 4 o'clock. She pulled out the report with all of the evidence against the Israeli 'mole' and organized and highlighted the most important points. Although she wouldn't have the opportunity to share it with Chairman Russell for three days, she may not have another golden opportunity to make a final review. She had put everything in order by 11:00 am. She unpacked and selected the outfits that she would wear to this week's galas. There was tonight's dinner, the all important Tuesday function where she had to dress conservatively for Chairman Russell and the final State Dinner on Friday. And then she'd go back to Phoenix next Saturday.

It wasn't until 1:30 pm that Cliff came back from the office.
"Where have you been?"
"Oh, you know how it is running the country and all."
"I know exactly how it is, so what took so long?"
"Listen to you; I've been a good boy. I was going through the reports from the AS Committee and I don't read as fast as you."
"OK, OK, the interrogation light is off. Let's get some lunch, I'm starved."
"I've got a nice quiet place that Bill told me about. They've got nice sandwiches or Italian for lunch."
"Sounds fine. Let's go"

Cliff led Pat into the Quilted Bear on Adams Street and asked for a table along the side and almost in the back of the room. By this time of the day, the restaurant was almost empty. As empty as any restaurant in Washington gets, that means about four or five other tables of diners. Cliff ordered a bottle of Cakebread Chardonnay. At first the waiter hesitated, then Cliff mentioned that Representative Baker had it stocked here and suggested that he try it.

Their chilled bottle arrived and the waiter poured the first glasses and took their order.

Pat tasted first. "What a fine tasting wine; very crisp."

"The advantages of taking restaurant suggestions from the Representative from California."

"So, are you going to get me drunk?"

"Guilty as charged."

"Normally, I wouldn't allow it, but since you're going to do it first class … well, it would be a sin to leave a drop of wine in this bottle."

"Cheers."

Cliff was charming. He looked at Pat with those light green eyes as he hadn't looked at her in years. He touched her briefly on her arm. He grabbed her hand when he made his points. They talked for hours; about everything, about anything. By the end of lunch she was rubbing his leg with her feet. His touch had become more deliberate, more passionate. They left the restaurant, got into a taxi and began groping each other like high school sweethearts. Without stopping to notice, they were back in their apartment. Pat jumped up on Cliff, hanging around his neck and shoved her tongue as far down his throat as she could. Cliff carried her to the bedroom and pitched her onto the bed. He began ripping his clothes off. Pat unbuttoned and wiggled until she was naked. Cliff flopped on the bed, almost on top of her. They kissed and clutched each other like it was their first time. Cliff was hard, Pat was wet. Softly, slowly Cliff slid his penis into Pat, inch by inch. When he was finally in, Pat rose up her legs and turned her pelvis up until he found her G spot. The rhythmic symphony began. Slowly, quietly at first, like the intro to a sonata. Then came the chorus. Her heart was beating fast, the movements were perfect. The chorus went on and on and on. Until she had reached the highest note in the symphony. She knew it. She could feel it. The crescendo was coming and nothing in the world could interfere with that now. Her heart stopped for a second; she twisted her body. She was gripping Cliff as if she had a third hand. He was pulsating inside of her. Once more she climbed with excitement and then continued with her pleasure ride. Wave after wave; feelings of warmth, security and satisfaction filled her being. Finally, the music receded. Cliff fell on the bed next to her. He looked exhausted. She smiled with satisfaction. Somewhere deep inside of her, the maestro took a bow.

It seemed like an eternity later that Cliff got up and went into the bathroom. She heard the shower begin to run. Cliff's cell phone rang. Where was it? It must be in his pile of clothes on the floor, but she was too tired to try to find it. Not two minutes later, it rang again. This time, Pat leaned over the side of the bed and worked through Cliff's clothes until she had uncovered it in his pants pocket. It had stopped ringing. Pat quickly worked through the menu to 'missed calls'. It was the same number twice. She recognized it. It's 'the trash'. She deleted the entries and put his phone back in his pocket. She dragged herself completely up onto the bed again. Something smelled. She took in a stronger breath through her nose. And then again against the sheets. It's the sheets! I've told Cliff twice a week isn't enough to have the housekeeper come. "Mondays and Thursdays are fine." He says. It's not.

She got up, showered and dressed for dinner. When she came out of the bedroom with her black laced dress with her black bustier underneath that increased her cleavage to the 'very interesting' level without reaching the 'total distraction' proportion, Cliff seemed distracted by something else. After a quick double-take of her outfit, he was with her again. They left by taxi to yet another onslaught of political maneuvering hidden behind beautiful smiles and perfectly scented cologne and perfume.

Sunday

Cliff and Pat woke up and had Sunday breakfast as they had so many times before. They spent most of the morning passing sections of *The Washington Post* back and forth to each other, sipping coffee and munching boiled eggs and biscuits. They dressed and were on their way to the First Baptist Church in the Lincoln Park district for the 11:00 am service.

Pat reviewed the crowd as they took their seats. After the final hymn, Pat was headed for the door to begin milling around the people who naturally gathered to congratulate the pastor on another fine sermon and mill around with people like Pat. Cliff caught up with Bill Baker and they went off to the side talking sports, bringing a reasonable number of men with them. The ones left in the group surrounding the pastor were the important ones, anyway. They were the seasoned veterans of the political game and didn't have time to check in on anyone else's sports activities. Pat spent almost as much time as the pastors service talking with as many people as she thought necessary. She was just finishing up with White House Chief-of-Staff, Robert McGannon. She mentioned to Bob, "You know, it's been hard to even spend time with Cliff. He's pretty tied up with the AS Committee and the whole 'mole' issue." She lowered her voice as she reached the end of her sentence. "Obviously, we're doing everything that we can. We've even set a trap."

"What kind of trap could you possible set for a spy, if you don't mind me asking?"

"Well, I doubt that you'll be applying for the job so, we've put out a job opening in State for a Hebrew translator. We're hoping that he or she will be looking for easier access to information. We'll check any current g-workers who apply."

"Good luck with that. And thanks for the tip; I won't apply for the State job. Take care Bob and send my best to Ada and the kids. I hope she's feeling better soon."

"Thanks Pat, I will."

She walked by the side of the entrance where Cliff remained with only a few stalwart Redskins fans discussing the possibilities for next season. They made their way to the car.

"What did you find out?" Pat started.

"I think we talked the 'Skins out of the Super Bowl next year."

"Cliff, how many times had I told you that every time you create your own little Sports Center discussion, you're missing golden opportunities to hear what the other branches of the government view as important?"

"I think I need to hear it one more time." Cliff smiled. Pat shook her head.

The afternoon was spotted with rains. Pat took the opportunity to re-read *How to Argue and Win Every Time* by Gerry Spence. It was amazing how someone whose political views were diametrically opposed to hers could help her so much. But every time she browsed through the book, she gleaned a little more of his winning style.

Cliff was a complete nuisance all afternoon. He thought that last night was going to continue all weekend. She was completely satisfied. But he kept prancing around grabbing her butt and trying to be playful with her breasts. She was never going to finish her book with him around. Finally, she slid down on the floor and gave him a blow job right there on the couch. She was done in five minutes and he was asleep in ten. Pat went back to reading her book.

By the time Cliff came to and washed up, Pat was ready to go out for dinner. She insisted on her favorite Japanese sushi place and Cliff was in no mood to argue. Sushi was always so fresh and clean to Pat. The lack of fresh sushi was one of the drawbacks to living in a land-locked State. It doesn't matter what anyone said, if the ocean wasn't a 'stones throw' away from the restaurant, Pat wasn't eating sushi. She had her rules and that was one of them. Cliff normally went for the tempura. Wimp. Anybody can fry. He'd go to a Japanese restaurant in Kansas—in fact, he probably has. But this is D.C. and the ocean is close enough. Dinner was excellent.

When they got back to the apartment, Pat changed into a cotton night dress and crawled into bed with her book. Cliff took the hint and stayed in the living room amusing himself with evening television. Pat was sitting in her bed with the book open and her eyes staring at the page, but she didn't read a word. Her thoughts were visiting tomorrow. She went over her plan from start to finish playing out each possible scenario that could impact successful insertion of the tapes. She dozed off with the book on her lap and the TV droning in the background.

Monday

Pat was losing her jet lag; she slept until six this morning. She and Cliff had scrambled eggs and biscuits for breakfast and spent hours discussing the issues involved with the Israel-Saudi Arabia negotiations. Cliff needed to keep a lid on the hawks in the AS Committee. Israel was not be fucked with no matter how much oil was at stake. Everyone needed to know that Saudi Arabia would use every drop of oil to eliminate Israel and didn't care that there would be none left to run the US war machine, much less the American taxpayers' car. Peace was the only way to maintain the Saudi pipeline and negotiation was the only way to peace. Cliff was primed and ready to go by 9:30.

As Pat was preparing to leave on her mission, Linda Wentworth called. Linda had arrived yesterday and wanted Pat to shop for a dress for her for the Dinner tomorrow night. Pat couldn't say 'no' to the Speaker's wife.

Pat and Linda had a wonderful time visiting most of the designer shops downtown, finally agreeing on a nice Armani number. It was a conservative, to-the-neck, long dress with a slit up the side to just above the knee. Linda is a full-figured woman, but Pat convinced her to give her cleavage a break and move the focus to her legs. The slit was nice but not high enough to reveal Linda's well-endowed thighs. It was perfect. Linda was so thrilled with the dress that she let Pat beg off lunch with only two, 'I have to go's.'

Pat had a leisurely lunch at the Watergate. Since her morning was shot, she'd have to wait until well after lunch to make sure that 'the trash' didn't come home for lunch. At about 1:30, Pat took a cab to 15th and New York Avenue. She walked quickly over to 1482. She entered the outdoor courtyard and made her way around to apartment J. It had an upper bolt and a standard door lock. She took a small tool kit from her purse and took out two small metal picks. Jamming one in place at the base of the lock, she maneuvered the other until she caught the bolt. She twisted it counterclock wise as the bolt slid out of the door jamb. The door lock was a breeze. She came in, shut the door behind her and locked the door handle again. She took a breath. She smiled to herself. Another thing Cliff doesn't know about her. When she was practicing 'picking locks', she had a five foot high two-by-four with about six different types of lock on it. She practiced for days, making sure that the movements were smooth and concise. She told Cliff that she was trying to decide on which set of locks to buy. She didn't buy any and Cliff never noticed. After that, she would notice the types of locks on the doors that she entered. She wanted to be sure that she could identify the lock type by sight.

Pat started to look around the apartment for a subtle place to leave the cassettes, but no too subtle. It had to be somewhere that 'the trash' wouldn't stumble across it over the next couple of days but somewhere that Special Ops would find it.

Like a crash, Pat heard the sound of keys in the lock of the door to the apartment. "Oh shit", she thought, "I've got to hide." Under the pull-out bed was too small and too much in the open; not the bathroom. She jumped into the closet and melted against the back wall. Her breathing got shallow as the sound of the door opening came roaring into the room and hit her chest like a brick. She was still. She could feel the movement of her body with every beat of her heart. The door shut; the brick hit her chest again. Pat could hear movement. She tried to think; what could she do if this closet door opens? Throw herself at the girl and run out? Hit her? She couldn't get away without being recognized. Maybe she could put something over her head; but that would make noise. "Wait", she thought. She heard a computer start up and the keyboard started clicking. There was no air to breathe. Her breathes were so shallow and she didn't dare inhale too much. She could hear the air whistle into her nose as she tried to bring more air to her lungs. But her chest was too tight. Nothing was moving except for the rhythmic sway that she felt in her body with every beat of her heart. The clicking stopped. The computer was shut down. Then she heard the door again. It closed solidly. The bolt slammed shut. For a moment, Pat couldn't move. Carefully, she pushed open the closet door. Fresher air rushed to her face. She took a medium sized breath. She trembled over to the bathroom and vomited into the toilet.

Two minutes later, Pat had wiped her face and finally taken her first deep breath. It was over; she had made it. She didn't get caught.

Pat looked around the room with less discerning eyes and selected the lower drawer of the night table. She slid the three small cassette tapes to the back of the drawer. Slowly, she entered the living area and tried to see out the windows. All seemed clear. She opened the door slightly at first and then slipped out, locking the door handle and then very carefully locking the bolt with her two metal picks.

Even out on the street, Pat didn't feel completely comfortable. And there were no cabs driving by this area. She walked up New York Avenue until she got to 14th Avenue and was able to hail a cab. She went to her upstairs flat for a little 'alone time', plus she didn't want any cabbie bringing her from that area to her apartment.

After an hour of reflection and calming, Pat walked from her flat to the apartment. The air made her feel good again. She felt alive. Walking along, the rush of the afternoon's excitement ran through her body. She was alive and everything was right with the world.

Cliff got home about 7:00 PM. Pat didn't even hesitate at opening a bottle of Merlot. Her body, her face and her eyes listened intently as Cliff recounted the events of his day. But her mind was flying.

Tuesday

D-Day. Today she understood how General Dwight D. Eisenhower felt when he took the biggest risk of his career. Adrenaline and fear ran through her body beyond the point of distraction. She was fidgety. She didn't dare drink any coffee today. She knew that composure was the most important thing and the thing hardest to maintain. But the 'troops' were looking to her for leadership. She needed to do her job and she needed to do it well.

'Buck up, soldier'.

Cliff had slipped out of the apartment unnoticed during one of her internal soliloquies. She went through her plans over and over again. She selected the papers with the information that would implicate Cheryl and rehearsed her speech to Chairman Russell until every word was perfect and every intonation was sincere.

She put the papers in the zipper portion of her purse and zipped it shut.

She wasn't hungry so she had a few pretzels to absorb the acid and provide her with some sugar.

Next, she looked at the outfit that she had selected for the evening. She tried it on. It was extremely conservative; a long dress without a slit, to the neck with long sleeves. She had selected it because it looked like something Scarlett O'Hara from *Gone with the Wind* would have worn. Now, it was for that same reason that she hated it. It was too feminine and no one was going to see Scarlett O'Hara shining through a dress.

Damn it, why couldn't she just wear pants and a jock-strap! It's the only thing these assholes listen to.

She went through her wardrobe again, piece by piece. Nothing low-cut, nothing with a slit, nothing short, nothing cute. Finally, she came across a black pants suit. The legs of the pants were large and when she stood still, it looked like it could have been a skirt. The coat was European cut but with a Nehru length that covered her butt completely. With a red sash wrapped similar to a tie, it was the perfect Victor/Victoria look.

Now, for her hair. She had to do something with that flip. There weren't many choices. The most effective was to wrap it into a low bun and cover it with a black crocheted scrunchie. She still had a few hairs hanging from her temples that provided definition to her face. It was the only real trace of femininity. That was fine, she's still a woman!

In full dress, Pat unzipped her inner purse and took out the papers as she once again ran through the discussion with Chairman Russell, showing the information on the papers for emphasis to her points. She practiced again. After the third practice run, she felt comfortable and convincing. She put the papers back into the zipper part of her purse and zipped it shut. She took off her outfit and grabbed a few more pretzels to get her through until dinner tonight.

When Cliff came home, Pat was standing in the kitchen in her thong underwear and bra munching pretzels. Cliff made some 'male noise' and walked over and grabbed her bare butt.

"P-l-e-a-s-e Clifford, grow up."

"What's wrong with you?"

"Nothing's wrong with me. I've had a helleva day and I don't want to talk about it. Now, let's just get dressed for dinner and get through this evening."

"Get through this evening—you make it sound like a task."

"It's work, Cliff. It's the most important work you'll do all day. It's the most important work I'll do all day."

"Yeah, yeah, yeah." And with that, they both began preparing for the evening.

Cliff showered first and took a quick shave. He moved into the bedroom, turned on the TV and slowly dressed during the commercial breaks of his shows.

Pat slipped out of her underwear and stepped into the shower. She started by shaving her armpits and soaping her entire body. She took her time as she shaved her legs from the ankle all the way up to the top of her thigh. She bent over to rinse her legs by hand. She stood up slowly, sliding her hands along her inner thighs until her thumbs were pressed against her pubis. The thought of power excited her. She kept her left thumb pressing against her pubis and moved her right hand to her breast and grabbed her nipple lightly between her thumb and middle finger and gently stroked it with her index finger. The thought of her wielding power almost made her wet. 'That's enough', she thought, 'just enough to keep the excitement level on par with the adrenaline.' She rinsed her body and stepped out of the shower. As she dried in front of the mirror, she couldn't help but smile to herself. This was going to be a night to remember.

Pat powdered, perfumed and got back into the outfit that she had worn for hours earlier that afternoon. She wrapped her hair into a bun and covered it with the black scrunchie. She tied her sash in a half Windsor but let the ends drop down evenly side-by-side. She stroked her temple hairs until they fell like book-ends to her face. She picked up her purse; she was ready.

Cliff finally put on his tuxedo jacket and turned off the TV. They were off.

The affair was an informal formal. Dinner would be served but the speeches would be kept to a minimum, only the President and the Chairman of the Armed Services Committee were scheduled, and dancing would be hosted by a live band.

Chairman Russell was greeting most people as they entered. When Cliff and Pat were greeted by the Chairman and his wife, Cynthia, Pat leaned over during her hug with the Chairman and whispered, "I know you'll save me a dance later." The Chairman had a slightly quizzical face when he leaned back from the hug, but immediately returned to his stern but friendly demeanor.

As they waited for all the guests to arrive, Cliff sought out Representative Baker. Pat found Linda Wentworth. It wasn't difficult; she was ravishing; and already the 'talk' of the dinner. "Linda, you look wonderful", Pat said as she walked closer to Linda, still taking in the full-bodied look from a distance. "Pat, I feel wonderful. Thanks so much for your help. I don't think the Speaker is going to make it through the speeches tonight; he hasn't been able to keep his hands off me."

"I think the Chairman has a suite of rooms available to the guests. I'm sure he wouldn't mind if you missed his speech as long as you came back for the dancing."

"Oh Pat, you are so bad. Thanks again, dear."

"OK, Linda, I'll see you on the dance floor."

"OK, dear."

Pat and Cliff settled down at their table for dinner and the speeches. The President stayed away from all of the 'hot' issues and took the opportunity to push his Education And Transition, E.A.T. He unveiled the slogan for his EAT program, 'feed your head'.

"Good God", Pat thought, "what is with these 'rock-n-roll' Presidents? Is 'Jefferson Airplane' the live band tonight? What ever happened to Presidents who didn't admit to smoking marijuana?"

Chairman Russell, on the other hand, attacked both Israel and Saudi Arabia for their disagreement and, as with every well-planned negotiation, threatened both Israel and Saudi Arabia with the use of United States military power to resolve the issues if they couldn't resolve them alone. Charles Russell was the perfect 'bad cop' for the negotiations. He commanded a Black Ops Unit during Vietnam and led the way for the 'Hawks' during Desert Storm and the invasions into Afghanistan and Iraq. Nobody believed that his speech was purely a negotiation ploy. He would spill blood tomorrow, if he could.

Finally, the dancing began. Chairman Russell wasted no time in asking Pat for a dance. Once on the dance floor, he started the conversation.

"Cindy tells me that I have two left feet, so I'm sure that you didn't want to just 'cut some rug' with me. What's on your mind?"

"Well, I think that you're doing fine. But I did want to talk to you privately.'

"The last woman who asked to see me privately later became my wife. Since that job's not open, what would we discuss?"

"I believe I found your mole." Chairman Russell pulled his head back revealing that quizzical face again.

"Cliff didn't say anything to me."

"Cliff doesn't know. Perhaps we could speak in more details privately."

After a long sigh, Chairman Russell said, "I have a suite available to me upstairs. Room 1865; be there in ten minutes."

"Thank you for the dance."

"The pleasure was all mine."

Pat made her way back to their table. Cliff was sitting alone looking bored yet still cruising the room with his eyes. She came back into his focus as she approached. She sat down and took a sip of Champagne. She took a larger sip. After five minutes of no conversation with Cliff, she leaned over and grabbed her purse. "I have to go to the Ladies Room." She saw Cliff nodding his head as she started towards the back of the room. She stopped at the lavatory outside of the elevators. Two minutes later she was on her way up to the 18th floor. The elevator doors opened. Pat took a deep breath and stepped out. Room 65 was to the left. Down the corridor she went. After two left turns she was at the door—Room 1865. She knocked; firm but not too loud.

"Come in, Pat" It was Chairman Russell.

She opened the door. She entered into the Living area of the suite. There were two sofas, a few chairs and the TV and stereo system along the wall to her right. In the middle of the room was a large mahogany desk behind which Chairman Russell sat talking on the phone. He motioned Pat to one of the chairs in front of the desk. She sat down. Chairman Russell finished his call and hung up the phone.

"Now, what's this all about?"

"There's an intern at the Interstate Commerce Commission with ties to radical Semitic groups here in the U.S. and she has been making regular reports back to Jerusalem. Look at these." Pat handed her documentation to Chairman Russell. He took the papers but without even looking at them, said, "My mole knows planned troop movements throughout the world, not which oil truck just entered Georgia. How can an ICC intern get classified military information?"

"She's sleeping with my husband."

"Cliff wouldn't ..."

"She's a twenty-two year old Arizona resident working in DC. She's an American. He'd trust her. He wouldn't consciously betray his country, but …'

"I can't believe that Cliff would say anything to anyone."

"I don't know if he'd say anything either. But look at her background." With that, Chairman Russell began reviewing the papers that he held in his hand. "Besides her College friends, look at the flights that she's taken; always at Congressional break times. Always three days in Jerusalem."

"Pat, if we followed up every lead from ordinary citizens …"

"Chuck, if I were an ordinary citizen, I wouldn't be sitting here talking with you."

"I'm going to need more proof than this."

"Then, get it!"

Chairman Russell snarled at Pat as he picked up the phone and punched in a series of numbers. "Diaz, Russell here. Any nibbles at the bait? Who?" Chairman Russell looked closely at the papers in his hand and looked up directly at Pat as he said, "Got it, Cheryl Chapin. Thanks." He hung up the phone. "Alright, we'll investigate her further. I'll let you know if we find anything."

"Thanks." Pat got up to leave.

"You know, Pat, this could get messy. If this implicates Cliff in any way, I'll take him out on the White House lawn and shoot him myself."

"Thank you Chairman. I'm sure that Cliff is an innocent conduit of information."

Pat walked out of the suite.

What had she done? What does Chairman Russell mean by 'implicates Cliff'? She all but told him that Cheryl might be using 'pillow talk' to get information. Maybe when they find the tapes … yes, that's it. When they find the tapes, it'll show that the information was obtained outside of the relationship with Cliff. But still, she felt unsure. This whole thing could blow up in her face. Depending on how Chairman Russell views his involvement, Cliff could be a traitor; a dead man.

Pat came back to an empty table and sat down. A minute later, Cliff sat down next to her. "What's wrong? You don't look so good."

"I don't feel so good. Can we go home?"

Wednesday

Pat had a fitful night. It seemed that time passed by her with every minute announcing its entry and exit. She turned from one side to the other and back again. Every time, she noticed Cliff sound asleep. It is true; ignorance is bliss. Sometime very early in the morning she must have fallen asleep because when six o'clock came around and Cliff got up to dress for work, Pat couldn't open her eyes, much less get up. Cliff told her that he had eaten and was walking out the door before Pat finally dragged herself out of bed.

Sure enough, the coffee was made and there were the remains of a bagel and cream cheese. Pat sat down to have a cup of coffee and try to think about last night. It was useless; there was nothing that she could do at this point. All of her cards had been played. Her plan had been perfect. Certainly it will work; the girl is as good as dead. But she had overlooked the effect of the zealous Chairman of the Armed Services Committee. 'How could I have missed that?' she berated herself. 'I know Chuck. I know that patriotism is a passion with him and he is passionate to the point of recklessness. I counted on that to trap the girl.'

But there is absolutely nothing for her to do now. Cliff's life and her political career are in the hands of this reckless patriot.

She began with the worst-case scenario. Cliff is implicated by the Chairman of the Armed Services Committee right in the middle of the negotiations with Israel and Saudi Arabia. Those negotiations are the only thing that will save a hanging in the press. The U.S. can't allow its allies and its negotiation partners to view it as compromised. The girl would 'disappear' and there would be no discussion of her extracurricular activities for Israel. News of Cliff's involvement would never hit the press. He'd be killed in an accident. Not quite as theatrical as Chuck promised, but he would be just as satisfied. *Shit, she'd better keep her distance from Cliff.* With Cliff gone, there would be a special election to fill his seat. And although she could fill his shoes, it seems unlikely that the party would back the wife of a traitor. Her career would be over.

The second scenario starts the same with the girl 'disappearing'. Cliff's involvement is seen as less than criminal but more than stupid. He would be told that he's retiring and won't be allowed to run for re-election. If he reacts, Chuck will pull out all the information about the girl and threaten him into submission. Cliff will know what happened but he may not know who or why. Regardless, her career would be over.

The third scenario starts the same with the girl 'disappearing'. Cliff's involvement would be seen as 'stupid and immature' He would lose the positions on all of the Committees that he works on and would be elected to seats on the Education Committee or Wildlife Preservation and Land Management Committee. For at least two terms he would be relegated to being 'a vote' and nothing more. Perhaps over time he could work his way back onto the Budget Committee, but the AS Committee and anything in NSA oversight would be out of reach. Her career would be put on hold and she'd have to fight just to get back in the game as a reserve player.

The only decent scenario starts the same with the girl 'disappearing'. Cliff has no involvement. The tapes clearly show that she was getting her information from a completely different source. His affair with her is incidental. The party leaves Cliff where he is and continues to support his re-elections. Everything continues without a ripple. Well, maybe just a little ripple. Since this was the only scenario that she foresaw, she would continue with her plan to leak the affair to the press when the girl 'disappears'. He'd be at the top of the police investigation interviewee list. He would be dodging bullets from every direction. His name and his face will be in every living room in the nation. And just when it is clear that he DID have an affair with this little intern, Pat will appear to support and stand by her man like Tammy Wynette never imagined possible. Then she'll sit back and see what happens. If the voters remain apathetic and continue to support him in his current position and his re-election, then she'll just let it be. But if they awake from their amoral-induced sleep long enough to call for Cliff to step down or seem unsure about their continued support for his re-election, then she will make her move. She'll have Cliff drop out of the re-election race. She'll spend the next two years building support for her run for Congress. She'll stay in the papers; working with non-profits for neglected or mistreated children or orphans; calling for more Medi-Care benefits; sniping at the incumbent. Then, she'll put it all on the line and let the chips fall where they may. If Arizona says 'no' to Mother Theresa, Ed McMahon and apple pie and re-elects that incompetent Representative, whoever he is, then she doesn't want to represent those ignorant, discriminating people. She could be just as happy divorcing Cliff, living off of his retirement money and maybe write her memoirs. Life could be so good. But it's all up to Chuck!

Pat finished her coffee with a piece of toast. Although awake, she still felt in a daze, just like she always did after a sleepless night. She went to the bathroom to shower and try to wake up. As she dropped her nightie off her shoulders and it dropped down to the floor, Pat caught sight of her naked profile. She stopped. She turned to face the mirror. It was still the familiar body that she knew, but she didn't look so good. Her face was haggard. As she leaned on the counter for a closer look, it seemed that her shoulders were rounded, her perky body had lost its luster, and attractiveness was the furthest thing from her mind. She felt and looked worse than when she had her period. She turned and took her rounded shoulders into the shower.

She went through all of the motions of taking a shower. As she walked out to the bathroom again, there was that same train wreck victim in the mirror again. She got dressed in shorts and a top. The weather was a little cool, but she wasn't going out today.

She tried reading, but even the newspaper wouldn't allow her to read more than the same paragraph over and over again. Television was no help either; inane talk shows or soap operas that were so far down the path to oblivion that it wasn't worth the effort to find out why Doctor Ritchie took nurse Jessie into the treatment room while her husband was in room 304 recovering from an automobile accident. She got up and went to the kitchen to brew some tea. A nice warm drink, a clear mind and peace and tranquility will follow. She tried. But the four scenarios slipped in and out of her partially conscious mind until she gave up all hope of meditating her way out of today.

Pat got up off the couch and went to the kitchen to fix lunch. She should have a light salad or soup and sandwich but like the death row inmate having her last meal, she grabbed a banana and the creamy peanut butter. She needed a grape soda just to get the peanut butter down her throat. Undaunted by the tiny voice in the back of her head telling her to stop this calorie-fest, she went directly to the corn chips and hot salsa. The bite of the salsa followed by the soothing flow of the grape soda was a constant cycle of punishment and exoneration.

The afternoon was a continuation of the morning with its complete distraction of her mind and there was nothing that would bring it into focus. Then the phone rang. Her heart jumped; she took a deep breath. "Hello, Pat Lewis here."

"Pat, this is Charles Russell. I was calling about that case that we were discussing the other night." Pat stopped breathing. "I pulled the file out so that I would get it right; it's in front of me now. You know, you were right, it was stolen merchandise. And I closed the case myself. I can't believe I forgot this case, but there's so many to remember."

"Of course," Pat said, "You can't remember them all. And this guy was working alone?"

"Oh yeah."

Pat nearly fell off her seat in relief. "Well, thanks for taking the time to follow-up on that, I appreciate it."

"Anytime Pat, if you need anything else just call me directly."

"Thank you, Chairman."

"Thanks Pat"

Pat hung up the phone with a squeal. She felt like she wanted to jump up and give a cheer, just like in College when the Home Team scored! Her best case scenario was unfolding! But she had to go through every step going forward; she couldn't afford to fuck up again. Every step had to have only one possible outcome—the one she wanted.

Cliff came home. Pat was set on having a celebration by herself ... and Cliff would be there too. So, she decided to go out for Italian food. They went to D'Amore. Pat ordered a bottle of Santa Margherita Pinot Grigio. She enjoyed all of it, the appetizers, dinner and desert. And of course, the wine. She was like a poor poker player, sitting with her royal flush and not able to keep the smile off of her face. All of this seemed to be lost on Cliff. On the way back home he commented, "I've never seen you eat like that before; appetizers and desert. What's up?"

"Nothing", she said with her Cheshire smile, "I was just hungry."

When they got home, Pat was exhausted. All that stress from waiting caught up with her. She went into the bedroom, undressed and put a robe on. She went into the bathroom for a shower. As she walked past the mirror, she dropped her robe off her back to the floor. She glanced to the side to glimpse her profile. She was vibrant! She continued into the shower and turned on the hot water. She began soaping up her body. She was tired, so she moved slowly. Her slow movements over her body became sensual. She spent more time rubbing her nipples than was necessary. She moved her right hand down between her legs and glanced past her clitoris. She was getting as hot as the water. Her breathing became heavy and sporadic. She continued exploring her body, slowly, lusciously. She was the instrument and the player, all at the same time. A glide of her right hand and a quiver ran through her body; a pinch by her left hand and she felt a twitch inside of her being. She enjoyed the power that she had over herself. A glide, a pinch, a glide, a pinch. But the next glide brought a quiver too strong to stop. She arched her back in pleasure as the hot water drowned out her soft moan. She stood there with her eyes closed and the water continuing to massage her recovering body. When she came back to the world with a deep breath, she climbed out of the shower and dried off. That face looking back at her was beautiful and satisfied. She picked up her robe, strolled into the bedroom and fell asleep.

Thursday

Pat was up early with Cliff to prepare him breakfast and see him off. She was sweet. And she would continue to be sweet and supportive for as long as it took. She sat at the table and began her detailed planning.

She would be out of Washington on Saturday at 11:05. In a couple of days she would make an anonymous call to the press regarding the affair between Cheryl and Cliff. It won't matter that the call is anonymous, reporters are vultures. They'll check it out, find out it's true and what could have been just another missing person in a city of missing persons will be front page news.

Cliff will ask for advice. She'll tell him to deny it. Nothing is more infuriating to reporters than having a taste of a story but not being able to make it stick. They'll press Cliff. They'll press the police. And, one way or another, they will dig until they hit pay dirt. By now the national news will have picked up the story. There's nothing more interesting than a politician who denies an affair. Everyone knows that they're fucking everybody, and the public likes to hear about it.

This whole time, Pat will stay away from Washington. It will give the press and the police the room to maneuver without her getting dirty. When the news goes national, they'll want to hear from her. And there she'll be, right by his side. Not admitting nor denying the affair and not admitting nor denying that he knows anything about the disappearance. Only that she supports her husband in everything that he does.

Eventually, he'll have to admit that he and Cheryl were more than friends at least once or twice during their friendship. But he will have complete and plausible deniability regarding her whereabouts. This will be the turning point. If his constituents believe him, he will keep his seat in the House and the whole thing will blow over before re-election and he'll win again. If they don't believe him, they may ask for his resignation or support will soften for his re-election campaign. Then Pat will step in and publicly denounce the actions of her husband but forgive him in front of the entire district—and probably the nation. She'll have the vote of every woman and gay man in the district. She'll continue the theme of forgiveness for him for as long as the reporters want to hear it. But every discussion will also include detailed support of the legislative work that Cliff accomplished and the impact that it made on his district. She'll send the message to the voters that we are of a like mind, but I am more moral than my husband.

But the best will come later. The first affair that Cliff has after they find Cheryl's body, Pat will walk up to Cliff, look him straight in the eye and say, "Remember what happened to Cheryl."

She smiled. Well, it was time to get her nails done; she had one more State Dinner tomorrow night. She thought that maybe she'd do her hair tomorrow and have a manicure and a pedicure today.

The Murderer

Tuesday

Staff Sergeant Anthony Malone sat on the couch in his two bedroom house, staring at the rum and coke in the glass that his right hand held. Here he was at 2000 hours getting loaded on rum and coke again. How did he get hooked on rum and coke, anyway? Oh yeah, it was that job in Haiti. He was waiting for the Nicaraguan attaché to show up at the hotel in Port Au Prince. He was sitting there for hours and was so bored that he finally asked for a drink, any drink. The bartender brought a rum and coke that he delivered with a big white-toothed smile. It was good. He ordered another. And another. By the time the attaché arrived he was almost drunk. Almost. If his C.O. saw him, he'd have been in the brig faster than he could say, "Sir, yes sir." It was nothing though. He grabbed the daily paper and walked towards the back. By the time he'd made his way to the kitchen of the hotel, the mark had ordered a late supper. He waited outside the kitchen door, knocked out the waiter when he came out with the tray on the rolling table. He had worn black pants and a white shirt, so he only had to take the bow tie to be in uniform, at least close enough to get in the door. He rolled the table up to the room. The mark opened the door and he walked in, rolling the table in front of him. He picked up the folded newspaper with his left hand and turned slightly to the left with a little wave of the paper. The mark took the bait. As he came closer he just slid his right hand inside the paper and pushed the knife out the other end and into his neck near the carotid artery. He just flipped open the paper as the blood started to spurt out so he didn't get a shower. The mark fell to the floor gurgling and holding his neck in a vain attempt not to die. He dropped the newspaper over the writhing body. He stepped to the side and walked into the bathroom. He cleaned the knife and checked for any little flecks of blood. 'Shit', he thought, 'there's blood all over my left wrist'. He washed his hands and tried to clean off the cuff of the shirt. It wasn't going to work. So, he rolled up his sleeve twice and it looked as good as new. He rolled up the other sleeve two times to match the left. He put the knife back in its sheath inside his pants, took off the tie and shoved it in his pocket. One last look and he walked back to the lobby bar. He ordered another rum and coke. The bartender served it with a big white-toothed smile. He drank it in three big gulps and he left the hotel.

He wasn't even sure of the day, maybe it was Tuesday. He'd been back for two weeks; kind of a cooling off period after each job. It was just a little too long. He was ready to get back to work.

Staff Sergeant Malone fixed himself another rum and coke and sat on the couch and began to stare into the glass. The silence was broken by the ring of the telephone. Staff Sergeant Malone jumped to his feet. He looked hard at the clock. It read 2130 hours. It was a habit of his to be aware of the time. He walked over to the phone and answered it.

"Staff Sergeant Malone"

"Anthony? This is Colonel Petroff, I need you in my office at 0800 hours tomorrow morning."

"Yes sir."

"Good. Be prepared."

"Yes sir."

Staff Sergeant Malone hung up the phone. A smile can over his face. He drank his rum and coke in three gulps and left the room.

Wednesday

Staff Sergeant Malone was waiting outside of Colonel Petroff's office at 0800 hours. Promptly, the Colonel's aide escorted him into the Colonel's office.

Colonel John "Black Jack" Petroff. "Black Jack" got his name and fame in Vietnam. He did three tours of duty; two of them with Special Ops. He left the war with 58 confirmed kills. Most of them assassinations. Most of them up close. Since then he'd been to Afghanistan, North Korea, Nicaragua, Colombia and Cuba.

Staff Sergeant Malone felt privileged to report to "Black Jack". He knew; he'd been there. Every mission that he'd been given, he knew that "Black Jack" understood the risks associated with each job. This was no fucking bureaucrat passing out death warrants to strengthen their political position. This was the real deal. This was an American legend whose only concern was to protect American freedoms.

He walked up to the desk and stood at attention.

Colonel Petroff saluted back and said, "At ease, Staff Sergeant. Sit down."

"Thank you, sir." He sat on the edge of the chair with his back straight, almost at attention.

"I've got a nasty one for you. We need to investigate a citizen who is suspected of providing intel to the Israelis."

"Yes, sir"

Colonel Petroff leaned forward and handed a piece of paper to Staff Sergeant Malone. "This is the address. I want you to head over there this morning and see if you can confirm our suspicions. She won't be there, she'll be at work."

"She?"

"Yes. One Cheryl Chapin. 24. You'll love this, she works in our government 9:00 to 5:00. But we suspect that she may be using her cunt instead of a microphone to gather information." Colonel Petroff blinked his eyes while nodding his head once and said, "See what you can find out."

"Yes, sir."

"Get back to me as soon as you can; before she falls off the face of the earth."

"Yes, sir." Staff Sergeant Malone stood up at attention and waited for a return salute. Colonel Petroff saluted and he turned and walked out of the office.

Staff Sergeant Malone went back to his house and changed into civvies and then took the M to 12th & F and walked the area around the apartment building of the mark. Once he was sure that nothing was out of order and the area was clear of unfriendlies, he made his way to apartment J. He worked the lock as quickly as if he'd had a key. He stepped inside. The apartment was small. It was L-shaped and he was at the corner. To the right was a kitchen that was half the depth of the apartment. Cabinets, a refrigerator, corner cabinets, a stove, another corner cabinet and a large cupboard surrounded a small table with two chairs in the middle of the room. Straight across from the kitchen was a couch. It was facing the kitchen, so he assumed that there was a bed that pulled out. Next to the bed was a small night table followed by an overstuffed chair. Across from the chair and past the kitchen was a long thin table against the wall that had a computer and a small television and a DVD player connected to it. The table butted up against a short wall behind which were a bathroom and a shower. Along the back wall of the apartment was a series of floor to ceiling closet doors.

Staff Sergeant Malone put on his plastic gloves and began an organized search of the apartment. After a one hour search he had only found three small cassette tapes that looked like they were used with a Dictaphone. He spent the next 90 minutes searching the files of her computer, downloading 45 selected files to his jump drive. The files all made references to a 'friend' who had 'influence'. With each one, Staff Sergeant Malone was getting more and more heated. Colonel Petroff was right again; this bitch was fucking information out of someone.

He checked out the side window. When the area was clear of citizens, he walked out of the apartment and locked the door behind him as quickly as if he'd had a key.

By 1215 hours, Staff Sergeant Malone was again waiting outside of Colonel Petroff's office. Again, the Colonel's aide escorted him into the Colonel's office.

He walked up to the desk and stood at attention.

Colonel Petroff saluted back and said, "At ease, Staff Sergeant. Sit down. What do you have?"

Staff Sergeant Malone took the three small cassette tapes out of his coat pocket and laid them on the desk. "I don't know if there's anything on these but I thought that we should check. They won't be missed."

He knew that 'Black Jack' understood that these tapes were found out of clear view therefore reducing the risk of the mark identifying them as missing.

He pulled his jump drive from his pants pocket and laid it on the table next to the tapes.

"She definitely had a mark." He said.

"Thank you, Staff Sergeant, that will be all for now. I'll contact you with further instructions."

"Yes, sir." Staff Sergeant Malone stood up at attention and waited for a return salute. Colonel Petroff saluted and he turned and walked out of the office.

By 1900 hours Staff Sergeant Malone was preparing his first rum and coke for the night but the phone rang before he could drink it.

"Staff Sergeant Malone"

"Anthony? This is Colonel Petroff, I need you in my office at 0800 hours tomorrow morning."

"Yes sir."

"Good. Be prepared."

"Yes sir."

Staff Sergeant Malone hung up the phone. A smile can over his face. He drank his rum and coke in three gulps and went out to the back yard. He'd have to dig the grave in his garden; this was a citizen.

Thursday

Staff Sergeant Malone was waiting outside of Colonel Petroff's office at 0800 hours.

The Colonel's aide escorted him into the Colonel's office.

He walked up to the desk and stood at attention.

Colonel Petroff saluted back and said, "At ease, Staff Sergeant. Sit down."

"Thank you, sir."

"Your mission was successful. The files were all related to her mark in the House, Representative Clifford Lewis, but that turned out to be nothing. The tapes, however, were excerpts of closed door meetings of the Armed Services Committee meetings that occurred last week. Apparently, you intercepted them before they could be forwarded. That means that they are time-sensitive. As soon as she finds out that she's been compromised, she'll fly."

At this point Colonel Petroff picked up a folder from his desk and handed it to Staff Sergeant Malone and continued. "This is the file on Cheryl Chapin. Take a good look at her picture. I need you to locate her and take the first opportunity available to neutralize her. We don't have time for anything intricate. Even if you have to compromise yourself, it is extremely important to take her before she disappears. Is that clear, Staff Sergeant?"

"Yes, sir."

"If anything does happen, I'll do everything I can to get you out of the country."

"Yes, sir. Thank you, sir."

"That will be all."

"Yes, sir." Staff Sergeant Malone stood up at attention and waited for a return salute. Colonel Petroff saluted and he turned and walked out of the office.

Staff Sergeant Malone needed to make a decision; from her file he knew that the mark worked at the Interstate Commerce Commission so he could either begin his search at the apartment or at the ICC Building. He opted for the apartment. "Black Jack" was overly concerned about her flight. It wouldn't do if he lost her right out of the box. Again he stopped by his house to change out of his uniform.

He took a taxi to 14th and New York Avenue and walked over to 1482 Apartment J. After checking for anyone who might be watching, he unlocked the door and walked into the small apartment. No one was there. He checked the apartment. Everything seemed to be in order; there was no sign that she was aware of anything. After checking the side window, he exited the apartment and locked the door.

His next stop was the Interstate Commerce Commission. If she was truly unaware, she would spend the day at work. He should be able to acquire and monitor the mark until he can encounter an opportunity to take her out. If she suspects anything, even his presence could set her flight in motion. He took up surveillance outside of the ICC Building by "playing tennis". He stationed himself on one street corner in sight of the front door. When he saw a female with the appropriate build and hair he would walk across the front of the building to take a closer look. Then he would station himself at the opposite corner waiting for the next possible mark and walk back to the original corner. This worked fine for the quiet hours in the morning but soon the noon hour was approaching. He went an extra block south and purchased a newspaper and set himself at the edge of the stairs on street level. The crowds came out for lunch. Staff Sergeant Malone meticulously searched the groups of people as they walked down the stairs and out onto the street. He focused exclusively on the eyes for recognition. There were a few that had put on sun glasses almost immediately even though it wasn't a particularly bright day. In those cases he evaluated the body type and build and lastly, the hair color and length. The hair was the easiest change to make and was completely unreliable for certain identification.

Staff Sergeant Malone was becoming concerned. The lunch crowds were thinning out and there was no sign of the mark. Had he missed something at the apartment? Was everything the same to buy the mark some time? "Fuck!" he mumbled under his breath. But there was nothing he could do. There was no reason to believe that she was tipped off; the odds were still in favor of waiting at her work. So, he waited.

As he waited, Staff Sergeant Malone tried to remember how many times he had done this. Waiting around for a mark to show their face; trying to remain invisible. He couldn't decide which was more difficult, to wait on the other side of the world where he was much less invisible but more comfortable that the mark was, in fact, an enemy of the American Way or waiting here in his home where he was just another face, but many times the mark's face was as American as his. It was difficult to imagine that so many Americans were working against our Government. So many times he had read about his marks in the newspaper after the fact. They seemed, he didn't know how to describe them; average, maybe. It wasn't like offing Osama Bin Laden when you could look into his eyes and see the evil; see the hate that he has for all Americans. When he looked into the eyes of his home marks all he saw was fear. He tried not to look into their eyes. After all, he was a soldier. He knew that he only had the information needed to complete his assignment. All of the details of their treachery were unnecessary to the mission. It was enough to know that the assignment came from "Black Jack". He was his C.O. He needed to believe in his C.O. just like he needed his men to believe in him when they were on assignment. This was a team—he was the one who closed the security leaks. That was all there was to it.

Damn, sometimes he thought too much.

For the return of the lunch crowd he walked across the street and off-center from the entrance doors. From there he scanned the possibles as they entered the building. If she skipped the morning and came back to work after lunch, at least she would be in the building with only one way out. He continued his surveillance until the last few stragglers came back in from lunch—still no mark. He went back to "playing tennis". He could see the scenario unfolding; he would stake out the work all day and the mark would have an eight hour head-start on him. She would certainly go directly to New York where she could blend in to a larger crowd and possibly take asylum at the Israeli embassy there. If he waits here all day, by the time he contacts "Black Jack" she'll be in the embassy and on her way home later tonight. His planning was interrupted by a female leaving the building. The build was reasonable close; he began his walk to the opposite corner. He reached the edge of the steps as the woman was two steps up. He glanced directly at her eyes. She was focused on the steps; he was focused at her eyes. They were right. He expanded his vision to include her face as he turned his head forward again. It was the mark. She was heading in the opposite direction that he was walking. He knew that she would walk to the corner and turn right for two blocks to catch the M. Without a break in stride or a telling look back, he continued walking to the corner and turned left. Once out of sight of her he took off his jacket and threw it on the first bench that he came to. He picked up his stride until he reached the second corner. He turned left and crossed the street to get a view of the M station as soon as possible. When the station was in sight, he slowed to an average pace. He needed to have her enter first. There was also the possibility that she stopped along the way. He needed to remain patient. He was almost to the corner when he saw her walk into sight. She was heading for the M. He picked up his pace a little, walked down the steps, bought a ticket to get him to 12th & F and continued through the turnstiles, entering his ticket in the front and picking up the stub on the other side. He walked down to the platform and stayed away from the mark. He knew where she was going, or at least he thought he did. The file said that that she was ending her assignment at the ICC by the end of the week. It was consistent with her behavior of leaving early. She'd have some last minute items to take care of on Thursday. As long as they didn't involve running around town, she should just head back to her apartment. He would be sure before he committed.

The train arrived. He entered two cars down from the mark and settled into a seat by the door. At each stop, he checked to make sure she stayed on. She did. At 12th & F he raised himself slowly as the train slowed to a stop. He made sure that she got off, and then he exited his car. They made their way up to the street. He was hoping that she would head north on 12th to H but she immediately went west towards 14th. He kept walking straight. He slowed his pace; there was always the possibility that she would cut up 13th to H and he didn't want to meet up with her on the way. When he reached H Street he slowed to a snail's pace. He waited. He took a few more steps and waited. He took a few more steps. There she was—there's the mark. She didn't even look his way, just kept on walking to New York Avenue. She made the left and went to her apartment. Now he was sure. This was not the behavior of a bird ready to fly. Everything was consistent with an oblivious mark. There was no need to go crashing in there, blow his cover and have to leave the country. He hated to leave the country. Always some bullshit assignment; working with friendlies who turn on us a few years later. Then you're back there to off the same guys you just worked with. It was fucked up. He'd stay home. No, he'd thought of a way to get in.

He went back to his house and put on his dress uniform and took the largest duffle-type bag he had and put a body bag in it. He carried the bag to the trunk of his car and drove back to New York Avenue. He parked across the street, just past the view of most of the apartments of the mark's complex. He got out and walked up to apartment J. He knocked at the door.

The mark opened the door with the security latch on.

"Cheryl Chapin?" he asked.

"Yes, I'm Cheryl."

"I have a message from Representative Lewis. May I come in?"

"Yes. Yes, please come in."

The door closed and then opened completely.

He came in and closed the door behind him, softly.

"Can I get you something to drink?" she asked.

"Ma'am." He said with a nod.

The mark turned towards the kitchen on the right; Staff Sergeant Malone lunged, leading with his left hand until it was around the right side of her face. His right hand was in place on the upper part of the back of her head. He finished this one lunging movement by pulling her chin back towards him with his left hand and pushing slightly downward with his right hand. He stepped back.

He knew she was dead before her body hit the floor.

Staff Sergeant Malone opened the door, walked out to his car, took the bag out of his trunk and went back to apartment J. The bag was mostly canvas with a strong plastic bottom and wheels on one end. He unzipped the bag and pulled out the body bag. He reached into his pocket and pulled out a pair of examination gloves. He took off his white gloves, put the exam gloves on and proceeded to place the body in its bag. He bent the legs so that she would fit into the duffle that he brought. He zipped up the body bag. He took the duffle bag and laid the strong plastic bottom next to the body bag. He gently lifted the top of the body and laid it on the duffle. He moved to the other side and gently lifted the folded legs onto the duffle bag. He pulled the canvas sides from under the body and stuffed the excess body bag inside the duffle bag. He zipped up the duffle bag. He took off the exam gloves, shoved them into his pocket and put his white, dress gloves on. He turned off all of the lights and waited in the dark with his bag.

After five minutes, Staff Sergeant Malone checked the side window, opened the door and carried his bag outside. He turned and locked the door behind him. Then he picked up one end of the bag and rolled it out of the apartment complex, across the street and carefully lifted it into the trunk of his car.

He drove back to his house and went inside. He changed his clothes and fixed himself a rum and coke. He drank it in three gulps and went out front to the car. He opened the trunk and carefully pulled out the duffle bag. He rolled it into his house, closed the front door and rolled the bag out the back door. He drug it over to the garden and unzipped the bag. He carefully pulled the body bag out of the duffle and slid it into the hole that he had dug last night. He went to the shed, grabbed his spade and began filling in the hole. He took the leftover dirt and spread it all along the border of the yard where he had a variety of different plants and flowers. When he was finished he put the spade away, picked up the duffle, zipped it shut and took it back inside the house.

He checked the time, 2035 hours. He picked up the phone to call his C.O.

"Colonel Petroff here."

"Yes, I just wanted you to know that I met up with my friend and she's with me."

"That's great, I'm glad you two can spend some time together. And if you have some time, stop by tomorrow and we'll talk more."

"That would be great."

"Thanks. Good night."

"Good night."

Staff Sergeant Malone hung up the phone. He would be at Colonel Petroff's office at 0800, just like he had ordered. "Black Jack" would decide how long the body would remain in his garden and when and where it would be dropped to be found by the police. He fixed himself a rum and coke, sat on his couch and stared at the glass that his right hand held.

The Patsy

10 days earlier

Representative Clifford Lewis flopped into the big leather chair in his office in the Cannon House Office Building just down the street from the Capitol Building. Representative Lewis was in his second term as Representative of the 1st District in Arizona. Before this, he had served as Arizona State Representative for two terms and Arizona State Senator for two terms. But nothing had prepared him for the day he just had. There is always so much bullshit to his job, meeting constituents who visit Washington with their little problems; other leaders who try to blackmail the country to obtain power in their own country. But this problem was critical. Israel and Saudi Arabia were ready to go to blows. And the U.S was in the middle. On one side was our most favored ally, mainly because there are so many rich and powerful Jewish men who are citizens of the United States but haven't left their homeland in their hearts. On the other side was the most reasonable oil-producing country in the Middle East. They held the fate of the American military in their hands. Without their oil and the oil of the nations that they influenced, America's military would come to a screeching halt. And to make things worse, Israel stopped playing like an ally. They have increased their intelligence activities in the United States and are getting better information and sooner than the Armed Services Committee that he just left.

Suddenly, the phone rang.
"Hello."
After a delay, "Hello."
"Cheryl?"
"Oh Cliff, yes, it's Cheryl."

"How did you reach me here?"

"I spoke with Barb; she'd said that you had to stop by your office tonight. I just kept trying."

"Yeah I did. But you're still lucky that you caught me because I only stopped for some reports that I left. I'm tired and I'm on my way home."

"I know it's late but I just had to talk with you."

"What's up?"

"I lost my job today."

"What?"

"Yeah, next Friday's my last day. Bob found out that I had completed my school requirements and he said that meant that I couldn't continue in the intern program any more."

"But you haven't graduated yet."

"I know. I told him that, but he said it didn't matter if the ceremony was outstanding, that technically, I had graduated. Then he called around and got a couple of people to agree with him."

"Well, I'm not sure what to say."

"Can you help me find something? If I have to go back to Howells, I might as well disappear from the face of the earth."

"I'm sure it's not that bad."

"When was the last time you were in Howells?"

"I visit there regularly to speak with my constituents. And it looks as if I may be visiting it with greater regularity."

"Don't even say that."

"I'm just kidding. Let me make some calls and see what I can do. Now get some sleep. I'll talk to you soon."

"Ooh, I love you."

"I love you too. Good night, Cheryl."

"Good night, Cliff."

Cliff hung up the phone. "Great! Now I'm losing the best piece of ass I've had in a long time."

Cheryl was good. It's hard to say that she's the best he's had. He's had so many. It seems that any level of power is an aphrodisiac. In State Government he'd had any number of campaign workers. All of them were young, slim and tight; just waiting for the opportunity to help with the election of their candidate. They'd work on their knees, on their back and, some, leaning over a chair. But when he came to Washington it was ridiculous. He could have anybody; single, girlfriend, wife; it didn't matter. And unlike some of his co-workers, Cliff had taken full advantage of the situation.

And then there was Pat. Patricia Arlene Teasdale Lewis; the college sweetheart that he married. Pat was seeking power for reasons that he couldn't even fathom. She was very good at the politics and enjoyed it so much more than he did. But she didn't seem to enjoy any of the side benefits. As far as he could tell, she'd never had an affair with anyone; never accepted any bribes or made any side money from his position. He just didn't get it. She worked all the time. Every State Dinner was a time of intrigue and political maneuvering. He went to the dinners to pick his next partner. Even when Pat accompanied him, he could still set up an appointment for later in the week. And Pat was pretty. But she was two years younger than Cliff. She couldn't compete with the twenty-something girls with butts like melons and their twenty pound tits. She came into town every couple of weeks and he always made sure that he fucked her at least once, but that was it. She never wanted it more than once, anyway.

The first time Pat caught him, he was scared. She was threatening to leave him and ruin his political career. He promised her everything. And he kept his promises for a long time. And then he didn't. And she found out again. But she didn't leave him. It didn't take too long to see that she wasn't going to leave him. She wanted his career as much as he did; maybe more. After that it was constant. He'd start banging someone, she'd find out and he'd break it off. It happened so often and she found out every time, finally when Cheryl came around, he decided to just stay with her. She had a great body, she wanted to do it all the time and she even let him do her in the ass. And now he was losing her and Pat had nothing to do with it. Unbelievable!

He had a long day ahead tomorrow; he'd better go home and get some rest.

9 days earlier

Another hectic day; Cliff had the Budget Oversight Committee meeting all morning. He dropped off the reports and assigned them to a staffer to review. He would need an update by next Monday so he had a working knowledge of the issues before next weeks' meeting. Pat will be in town this weekend, maybe she can help decipher this crap. Barbara Gomez took the reports and assured him the staffers' review would be complete by Friday.

He picked up the reports for the Armed Services Committee meeting and he was off.

At least they served lunch at the AS Committee meeting. It was the least they could do; they have been monopolizing his time ever since the crisis began. Not that he was complaining; it was his job. And he liked the fact that he was one of the few people in the country who had access to confidential material and could possibly have input to the resolution of the impasse.

The whole thing started during the most recent conflict with Lebanon. According to the Israelis, a minor offensive of a tank battalion got bogged down pretty well. Even they admit that they were caught out of place. They needed to provide air support immediately and had to scramble available aircraft from the Sinai region. To keep the operation from going south before air support arrived, they fired a cruise missile from the battleship Meier in the Red Sea. The cruise missile traveled over Saudi airspace to its target, but it was an obvious treaty violation. And Israel didn't even to bother to advise the Saudis of the launch much less ask permission to use their airspace.

The Saudi's responded by accusing Israel of being reckless, citing the thousands of worshippers in Mecca who watched in fear as the missile flew just overhead. They immediately rescinded their support for Israel and closed access to the Red Sea, the Gulf of Aden and the Arabian Sea to secure their water borders from the 'reckless menace', as Israel is now commonly referred to by the Saudi Government.

Israel threatened retaliation for this assault by Saudi Arabia on the security of the Israeli Nation. That's when the United States stepped in and it's been nothing but a constant shuttle between Riyadh and Tel Aviv for the diplomatic corps; and a series of discussions, resolutions and strategies in the House, the Senate and in Committee.

This evening the discussions went well into the night. Dinner was brought in and the meeting continued past 8 o'clock. He would have to be back here again at 8 o'clock in the morning. Cliff went back to the apartment, had a quick bite and fell asleep.

8 days earlier

Cliff woke up late but hurried to arrive at the AS Committee meeting on time. His apartment was just down the street from the Capitol Building and it probably saved time to walk and not have to deal with the traffic. Thankfully, they provided a continental breakfast; otherwise he wouldn't have had anything.

Today, they went through their new strategy. The jist of the plan was to continue to allow the Israeli Navy access to the Indian Ocean by circumnavigating around South Africa and through the Mediterranean Sea. Supply ships that were not equipped with cruise missiles would be allowed to transverse through the Red Sea and the Arabian Sea to re-supply the cruisers and battleships in the Indian Ocean. The discussions were bogged down by the tribute to be paid by Israel for the services of the use of these waterways. It actually started with the disagreement that any tribute was due. These were not territorial waters owned by Saudi Arabia; and other countries, including the United States were free to use them with little resistance.

The problem was certainly complex. Israel was already paying whatever the Saudis said the going rate was for a barrel of crude oil; as was the United States. Now, for no truly valid reason, Saudi Arabia decides to close access to their nearest waterways. Had it been Iran or Iraq closing waterways, the United States would have sent in the Marines, taken over the operation of the country thereby maintaining the flow of oil to the US from that country and keeping the waterways open for its allies. But because it was Saudi Arabia making the move, the US military was frozen; at least for now. Nobody had a plan for overtaking Saudi Arabia. Certainly, they have been corrupted by the power their oil has wielded and have become 'soft' due to the pleasures that their money can buy in a capitalist environment. They remained the richest and most powerful oil producing country in the world; and the most prolific purchaser of American military hardware. Therein lies the problem. Just like Saddam Hussein and the Taliban in the 80's, America had once again equipped its ally to the point that it no longer needed America as an ally.

So, why would Israel pay tribute for the use of non-territorial waterways? If they did, Saudi Arabia could close something else off and demand a ransom for its services. This would be nothing short of bleeding the Israeli economy until it reached a point where it couldn't maintain the military resources necessary to defend itself. Israel would never accept the proposal.

On the other hand, Saudi Arabia was flexing its muscles and some accommodation needed to be made. If nothing else, America needed time to evaluate the Saudi situation. With its military already stretched due to Iraq and Afghanistan, as well as the standard commitments to South Korea, NATO and SEATO; there were few resources to address a conflict with the Saudis. And what was the motivation for this move against Israel? Who was behind it? Maybe a well placed Black Op could put an end to this whole thing.

Shortly after dinner, the Committee decided to break with no resolution to its newest strategy. Cliff headed home. It was raining. As he was walking up to his apartment, he noticed movement across the street. Someone was running towards him.

"Cheryl?! What are you doing here? Look at you, you're soaked. Come on, let's get inside."

He grabbed her right arm and moved quickly into the apartment before any of the neighbors could see them together.

Once inside the door, Cliff said, "Let me take off your coat. There; now go into the bathroom and take off those clothes and go dry yourself."

"Cliff," she grabbed at his lapels, "tell me you got me a job. I can't go back to Howells. Tell me."

"I'll tell you, but first, go dry off. And put on some of my clothes. I'll fix us a drink."

Cliff put his wet coat away, shook off the lingering rain from his hair and walked over to the wet bar at the end of the living room. He was bringing two bourbon and sodas to the sofa when Cheryl entered from the bedroom. She was wearing one of his ties.

"It was the only thing that fit."

"Cheryl. Here, let me help you."

Cliff walked toward her. He was already getting hard. Cheryl was so sexy and the tie hanging between those big breasts was too much to ignore. When he reached her he grabbed the tie and continued through the door-way into the bedroom. Like a well trained pet, Cheryl followed the tie onto the bed. Cliff began taking off his clothes. Cheryl threw back the cov-ers and lay on the sheet. Cliff was ready and entered her immediately. She was still wet inside. She grabbed his member tightly with her third hand. Cliff thrust his hips forward again and again; each time enjoying the resis-tance and the slight rubbing on the head of his penis. He could have kept going for hours but Cheryl swung her left leg around his hip. It was a motion he knew well; she wanted to be on top. They flipped without skip-ping a beat. Cheryl was spectacular. She wiggled and then leaned back as far as she could. Just as Cheryl was climaxing she leaned down and grabbed his left nipple with her mouth. He was over the edge. He couldn't stop. He began thrusting. They came quicker and with less care. Then he felt a pulsing deep within his being and it expended itself through his penis. Cheryl fell on his spent body.

Cheryl rolled over; sweat dripping off her glistening body. "I need to dry off again."

"More than that, we need a shower. Let's go."

"Wait, tell me. Tell me everything."

"Tell you what?"

"Tell me what you found for me."

Cliff hesitated. "I haven't found anything, yet."

"You said …"

"What? You're standing in the doorway, soaking wet, catching a cold and I told you to dry off and we'd talk. We're talking."

"You said you'd tell me."

"I told you.… look, I've been in committee for two days. I haven't had a minute to myself. I'll do what I can, but you knew this day was coming."

"You don't understand." Cheryl said getting up from the bed. Cliff rolled over and tried to grab her hand.

"Don't touch me." Cheryl stormed into the bathroom.

Cliff was unsure; what had just happened? What did she expect of me? He got up, put on a robe and went out to the Living Room to cut off her escape. She came out of the Bathroom door faster than he expected.

"Cheryl." He walked toward her

"You don't understand' she stiff-armed him and went directly to the front door. She grabbed her still wet coat and walked outside.

Cliff sat down on the couch. He leaned forward and grabbed one of the bourbon and sodas, covered with sweat from sitting out so long. He shook his head as he took his first drink.

7 days earlier

Once again at 8 o'clock Cliff was in Committee having another Continental breakfast. The discussions continued to work toward resolution to a new strategy. It was imperative that Israel maintain the right to access the international waterways. But for the time being, it seemed to be a better negotiating strategy to limit that access to ships with standard armaments. Eventually, the Israeli supporters won the point of contention and it was agreed that no tribute would be paid for this access. The US negotiators would convince the Saudis that their demands were excessive and that the issue was, and is, the use of cruise missiles; nothing else. The Israelis will need to be convinced that they will be held accountable for their inattentive actions. The US would never refer to the Israeli's as reckless.

As for the issue of Israeli intelligence against the US, one of the sub-Committees reported that they had set a trap to catch the mole and that since the AS Committee will be waiting for a response to its strategy, a delay of further Committee meetings will provide time for the trap to spring.

With a strategy to provide to the diplomats, the AS Committee adjourned until a response was received from all parties involved. It was time for lunch. Cliff caught up with Representative William Baker from the 5th District in California. "Hey Bill, where are you going for lunch?"

"I've got a great place for you, c'mon."

They went out the doors of the Capitol Building with Bill leading the way.

"Cliff, isn't Pat coming into town soon?"

"Yeah, she gets in tomorrow"

"Whoops, there goes your sex life."

"Tell me about it. And its worst than that; I found out that Cheryl lost her job at ICC. By next Friday she's out of here and back in Howells, Arizona."

"Oh man! Do they even have a hotel in Howells?"

"Very funny. She wants me to find her a job so she can stay in Washington. That would be great, but I don't know anyone who owes me that big a favor."

"And even if you did; explain to Pat how you used a 'chip' for Cheryl." Cliff laughed lightly.

Bill continued. "But I have a friend in the Justice Department. Do you want me to call over there and see if I can do anything? I'll do it if you think she's worth it."

"Well, it'd be a lot easier to keep her here than to find someone new."

"Oh, please!"

"You know what I mean, someone regular. I can get anyone for a night. Shit, even you can get anyone for a night."

They both laughed as they entered the Quilted Bear restaurant.

"O.K., I'll make the call this afternoon. You're going to love this place. The best part is that they stock Cakebread Chardonnay and Merlot especially for me. If you're ever here, just order it and tell them that I gave you authority to access my private stock."

"Thanks Bill. I could use a drink today."

"Well then, let's sit down over here."

The afternoon was filled with staffers and trying to catch up on all the administrative issues that had fallen behind over the past week. Bill called late in the day. The call was in but it would be a few days before he would know anything. Cliff thanked Bill. At least that gave him something to bring to Cheryl. And tonight would be the last opportunity that he would have to nail her. With Pat coming in tomorrow and staying all week, and the possibility of finding Cheryl a job by next Friday being absolutely miniscule; he wouldn't have an evening free before Cheryl left for home. He decided to stop by her place on his way to the apartment this evening and see if he could have her one more time before she left.

Cliff took a taxi to New York and St. James and walked over to 1482 New York Avenue as he'd done so many times before. He walked up to the door of apartment J and knocked. He checked the side window just in time to see Cheryl's face break into a smile.

She opened the door. Cliff flashed a smile and walked into her little place. "Cheryl, I'm sorry."

"I'm sorry, too. It's all my fault."

"No, I know that this is important to you."

"No, really, I didn't give you a chance to talk. It's just that.... forget it." Cheryl fell on him with her arms falling around his neck. Cliff kissed her softly on the cheek and whispered in her ear, "I made a few calls and there may be something in the Justice Department."

"Oooh." Cheryl jumped up and down.

"Maybe. I don't have any promises"

"I know. I'm just happy that you took the time to help me. And, I want you to know, that I put in an application with State for a translator job"

"Very good"

Cheryl jumped up and forward and landed in Cliff's arms again. They kissed. And then ... they kissed. Cliff felt Cheryl as she melted in his arms. As she melted, he grew hard. He wanted to move slowly; to enjoy what may be their last time together. But his body told him to move quickly. He slid his hands up and underneath the jersey that she was wearing. No bra. This is too good. He slid his right hand down her backside and into her sweatpants. No underwear. Keeping his lips locked to hers, anchored by his tongue, he switched hands; bringing his right hand up and under her jersey and moving his left hand down the front of her sweatpants and immediately slipped his middle finger into her pussy. It was wet. She helped him take off her jersey. Her tits slapped against his chest. He broke his mouth away from hers and crouched slightly to put her right nipple into his mouth as both his hands grabbed the waist of her sweatpants and moved them slowly to the floor. He crouched further to drop her pants all the way to the floor and took the opportunity to kiss and lick her pussy. He stood up slowly, moving to the right to suck on her left tit.

Cheryl unhooked Cliff's belt and unhooked his pants. She moved quickly down to her knees bringing his pants and underpants to the floor with her. She began to suck his cock while he threw off his tie, unbuttoned his shirt and threw off his undershirt. Cheryl looked up at Cliff's naked body and laughed deliciously. They moved to the couch. Cheryl lied down. Cliff gently lowered himself on top of her and entered her easily. But his rhythmic motions became quick and hard; pushing Cheryl's body further and further up the couch until her head was jammed against the armrest. With a final slamming thrust Cliff arched his back. Cheryl had nowhere else to go, so she shifted to the side, glanced off the armrest and the two bodies slid off the couch and onto the floor as Cliff continued in his arching with little thrusts against her pelvis. Cliff rolled off of her and lied exhausted on the floor.

After a few minutes of recovery, he looked over at Cheryl. She looked like she was asleep. He sat up and looked closer. She was asleep.

Cliff got up and found all of the clothes that he had thrown around and got dressed. He leaned over Cheryl's lifeless body and kissed her gently on the forehead. He locked the door handle and locked the door as he shut it behind him.

6 days earlier

With the AS Committee on an unexpected hold, Cliff was relatively free to continue to play catch-up with the other issues faced by his office. He called Barbara to send in the staffer who received the Budget reports three days ago. He knew it was going to be Karen. Karen McCormick was the great grand-daughter of old man McCormick who was one of the first to sub-divide his ranch in Scottsdale. He made millions in the transaction. That allowed Karen to receive a top-notch education; summa cum laude from Stanford and a Master's in accounting from Arizona State University. And she wasn't ugly. She had shoulder length brown hair that she normally wore in a bun. She had fair skin and light blue eyes. Her body was average; a little bit of a butt; hips not too big and tiny little tits. Although she wasn't Cliff's type, he always enjoyed meeting with her. She was always so clean looking and she smelled great. Sometimes he would fantasize what it would be like to undo that bun. But she was all work. And she was smart. It may have taken him a few times to understand everything that she was saying, but she always had a complete handle on the important issues.

Karen came in with her standard salutation, "Good morning, Representative."

She was wearing a black skirt, just above the knee and a white, cashmere sweater top. Boy, if he could see someone like Cheryl in that top; she'd stretch that cashmere into something worth looking at. Karen's little titties were completely lost in there somewhere.

"Good morning, Karen."

Just as they were starting, Barbara was on the intercom.

"There's a call for you, Representative."

"Thanks, Barb." He punched the button to line one. "Hello?"

"Hi Cliff, it's me."

"Just a minute." He placed his hand over the receiver and whispered to Karen, "Could you wait outside? This will only take a minute. Thanks."

Cliff watched as Karen got up from the desk and closed the door to the office behind her. She had a nice behind.

"Cheryl"

"Cliff, I just wanted to call to thank you for coming by last night. It meant a lot to me."

"I know."

"How did you get out of the AS meeting today?"

"Oh, they've set some sort of trap to try and catch the mole. We're 'on hold' until they come up with something. Look, I'm going to be tied up for a while. Pat is flying in this afternoon and she'll be here all week."

"Well, shit, I was glad that you were out of the AS meetings and now I get hit with the wicked witch of the West."

"Cheryl, please."

"Well, what about the Justice job? How am I going to know what's going on if you're out of commission? When am I going to see you next? I have to see you again."

"As soon as I hear anything on the Justice job, I'll have my office send an e-mail to your ICC address. And, believe me, if there's any chance that I can get away, I'll send word. It may just be a date and time, but you'll be there for me, won't you?"

"Oh, I'll be there alright, wearing your tie."

"Please don't remind me about the tie."

"I am sorry about that."

"You can make it up to me. I gotta go."

"I love you."

"Bye."

Cliff called Karen back into the office. She sat down and began her explanation of the issues raised by the recent modifications to the proposed budget. Cliff tried to keep his mind on the numbers but every once in a while he would get a whiff of her and he was immediately distracted. He loved the distractions.

Cliff spent the morning being distracted by Karen. But he took the opportunity with the information that he had just learned to have a working lunch with a few members of the Budget Committee to discuss some of the issues that Karen brought to light. They weren't as well versed on the proposal as Cliff and suggested that he bring up these concerns at the meeting next week for all to hear and review. Cliff felt pretty good with that trump. He stopped by and gave a quick 'thank you' to sweet smelling Karen. She responded with a small pout borne out of pride and thanked him for stopping by.

Cliff hurried through the afternoon in order to get home in time to meet with Pat. He didn't want to stay late and keep her waiting, otherwise she might get pissed off and that's no way to start a week with her.

When he came home to the apartment, it was to an empty apartment. Pat hadn't arrived. It was a bit unusual; she normally is in by now. After about a half an hour, Pat arrived with her two bags. He helped her in with her bags and began his greetings, "Welcome back."

"Well, you're in early", she said.

"I came home early to welcome you. Where have you been?"

"Oh, flight delays, heavy traffic, you know."

Cliff was set back by that remark. He knew it showed all over his face, but there was nothing he could do. Were his excuses so transparent that Pat turns them into a joke? He felt naked in front of her.

"Have you had dinner?" he asked sheepishly. "I thought we could get some good Italian."

"No, I haven't eaten, but I'd rather eat in. I'm a little tired so I may turn in early."

They agreed on Thai take-out. Cliff offered to run out and pick it up; anything to get out and away from this situation. Cliff brought dinner back and put the servings on plates and prepared a couple of beers. Pat came out from the bathroom and joined him. He wasn't interested in too much conversation after the bite he took earlier. Thank goodness, Pat wasn't interested in chewing off any more. They ate quietly. After dinner Pat went to bed, complaining of 'jet lag'. Cliff cleaned up the dishes and went into the living room to watch some television before he joined her in bed.

5 days earlier

Cliff woke up just after 6:00am and Pat was already up. Not too unusual; she was normally up early the first morning. She prepared him the best breakfast that he'd had all week. He went to the office but promised to return in time for lunch

It was almost 1:30pm by the time he did get home.

"Where have you been?" Pat sounded playful, so Cliff responded.

"Oh, you know how it is running the country and all."

"I know exactly how it is, so what took so long?"

"Listen to you; I've been a good boy. I was going through the reports from the AS Committee and I don't read as fast as you."

"OK, OK, the interrogation light is off. Let's get some lunch, I'm starved."

"I've got a nice quiet place that Bill told me about. They've got nice sandwiches or Italian for lunch."

"Sounds fine. Let's go"

Cliff led Pat into the Quilted Bear on Adams Street and asked for a table along the side and almost in the back of the room. By this time of the day, the restaurant was almost empty. As empty as any restaurant in Washington gets, that means about four or five other tables of diners. Cliff ordered a bottle of Cakebread Chardonnay. At first the waiter hesitated, then Cliff mentioned that Representative Baker had it stocked here and suggested that he try it.

Their chilled bottle arrived and the waiter poured the first glasses and took their order.

Pat tasted first. "What a fine tasting wine; very crisp."

"The advantages of taking restaurant suggestions from the Representative from California."

"So, are you going to get me drunk?"

"Guilty as charged."

"Normally, I wouldn't allow it, but since you're going to do it first class … well, it would be a sin to leave a drop of wine in this bottle."

"Cheers."

But it was Cliff who got drunk. He couldn't help but become very relaxed. And when he was relaxed he couldn't keep his hands off any woman within twenty feet. Today it happened to be Pat. He kept drinking and talking until he felt her leg rubbing his. He knew he was nearing pay-dirt. He became more aggressive. He needed to get her out of there and into anything that resembled a bed as soon as possible. They walked out arm-in-arm and grabbed the first taxi that came by. Cliff went for the homerun in the backseat. He shoved his hands up her blouse and worked through her bra until he was grabbing her tits. He gave her a long, wet kiss. She was responding, but not fast enough to do it in the car. They were at the apartment before he wanted to be there. So, he continued his attack as he inched her into the apartment. Once inside, Pat finally responded completely, jumping on top of him and kissing him back with her own long, wet kiss. He carried her into the bedroom and threw her on the bed. She bounced against the mattress. He began ripping his clothes off. Pat unbuttoned and wiggled until she was naked. Cliff did a swan dive onto the bed and just missed landing directly on top of Pat. He continued his assault on her mouth and when he thought that he had given her enough time, he entered her. Pat wrapped legs up and around him. She seemed to like that position. He started a swaying motion that was almost second nature to him. It was the "Pat" motion. She liked it and he always got off. Sure enough, after a few minutes, Pat twisted her body and the orgasm had begun. She wrapped her legs a little tighter and the tightness of her entire body became too much for him to take. He came; squirting a little more of his life-juice with every sway. Cliff fell on the bed next to her. He felt pretty good.

He must have fallen asleep. But he got up in plenty of time to get ready for dinner. He got up and went in the shower while Pat was still sleeping. He came out of the bathroom and found Pat up and around. She went in to shower and took her clothes with her into the bathroom. While he was dressing, his cell phone rang.

"This is Cliff."

"Cliff, it's Cheryl."

"I'm getting dressed for dinner; can I call you back, later?"

"Cliff, I saw you and Pat today in the restaurant. I thought the husband-wife thing was for the press and your congressional buddies. I didn't see either of them this afternoon."

"What? You're talking nonsense. I don't have time for this right now."

"I need an explanation."

"Well, I guess I'll have to explain it later, when it makes more sense. Don't call me again. I told you, you can't call me this week."

"Cliff"

"Good bye"

Cliff was annoyed. He told Cheryl not to call him. He told Cheryl that Pat was in town all week. If she were staying around, that would be one thing, but Cheryl was all but gone and there was nothing he could do about that.

Pat came out wearing a nice black dress. She looked great. He immediately forgot about Cheryl and escorted Pat to the door.

4 days earlier

Cliff and Pat woke up and had Sunday breakfast as they had so many times before. They spent most of the morning passing sections of *The Washington Post* back and forth to each other, sipping coffee and munching boiled eggs and biscuits. They dressed and were on their way to the First Baptist Church in the Lincoln Park district for the 11:00 am service.

As they were taking their seats in one of the middle pews, Cliff caught sight of Bill Baker. He gave him a quick wave and knew that he'd have someone to talk to while Pat was playing her political games after the service.

The reading was from Genesis; the story of Cain and Abel. A pretty accurate description of murder in Cliff's mind; one brother kills another over a bruised ego. Even today, in over 60% of the murders, the victim knows the murderer. Some things never change. That wasn't the point that the pastor wanted to make, but Cliff didn't stay awake long enough to hear what his point was. An elbow in the side and Cliff was awake and came back to the service slowly as they sang the closing hymn.

Outside, Cliff congratulated the pastor and stepped to the side of the steps where Bill and a few others were congregating.

"Hey, Bill, what do you know?"

"Not much my friend; another day in DreamLand"

"Did you ever hear anything back on the Justice job?"

"Sorry guy, I don't think there's anything in the cards there."

"It's OK. Thanks for trying."

"So, what are you going to do?"

"Not much. Cheryl will go back to Howells. I'll try to hook up with her there when I can. But I'll have to start looking around for something fresh."

"You know, I went out with Penny Johnson. Do you know her?"

"No."

"She's an assistant in Senator Golden's office. She's no 'looker' like Cheryl, but she's got a cute face, she's a little pudgy and she's got a great pair of tits. That's how I noticed her. I stopped into Brad's office and they were practically lying on the desk in front of me."

"How was she?"

"She gives great 'head'. But she didn't want to do anything else. She said she had a headache. I guess I'm not surprised … the way she was banging it against my cock."

"Yeah, that's really funny, Bill. Look, I can get 'head' any day of the week. I'm looking for more."

"You want a relationship!?"

Cliff glanced over to Pat. "I have a relationship, I'm looking for sex."

"Well, good luck. You may have to wait for fall when the new crop comes in."

"Fall is a long way off."

"You have to plan if you're going to have a good season. Look at the Redskins. They've already got their scouting reports in for the draft. They're planning to pick up a top quarterback. No top quarterback has taken the job since Joe Theismann because the 'Skins can't protect him. And they haven't had a good team since Theismann got his leg broken."

"Bill, you must have been ten years old when Theismann got his leg broken. You're talking about ancient history."

"I'm talking about history repeating itself. I predict the 'Skins will have a good season until the quarterback they pick up gets the shit kicked out of him and then everyone in Washington will be watching the playoff from their living rooms."

"O.K., you got me there; another season, another below .500 performance. Good prediction! It looks like Pat has about sucked the lifeblood out of everyone worth sucking. Here she comes. I'll see you tomorrow."

"Keep your head high!"

"Thanks."

Cliff walked out to meet Pat on her way over to pick him up. They made their way to the car.

"What did you find out?" Pat started.

"I think we talked the 'Skins out of the Super Bowl next year."

"Cliff, how many times have I told you that every time you create your own little Sports Center discussion, you're missing golden opportunities to hear what the other branches of the government view as important?"

"I think I need to hear it one more time." Cliff smiled. Pat shook her head.

When they got home Pat started reading a book. Cliff figured he'd make the best of a bad situation. If all he was going to have for the next week was Pat; then he'd have Pat. He sat down on the couch next to her and started petting her butt. When she shifted over and raised her butt a little, he took the opportunity to slide his hand right under her before she could settle back down. She sat on his hand with a start. She gave him a look of annoyance as she raised up again and he brought his hand out from underneath her. Her look didn't matter. Just like, 'there's no bad press'; 'there's no bad attention'. He moved his hand up to the front of her blouse and started flicking her nipple with his index finger. Pat shifted slightly. He moved the finger over to the other nipple and continued flicking over there. He came back to the left breast, then over to the right one. Eventually, Pat closed her book, put it down and carefully opened her blouse. She shifted up her bra, exposing her breasts to Cliff. He immediately took one into his mouth. Pat was undoing the belt and zipper of his pants as he shifted from one breast to the other sucking as hard as he could. Pat lightly pushed on Cliff's upper body to lie down backwards on the couch and she slid down to the floor and leaned over his crotch. She grabbed his throbbing member in her right hand and began gently licking and stroking up and down. After a few moments of anticipatory ecstasy, Pat shifted to the right and brought her left hand into the fray, lightly cupping his balls in her left hand. He could feel as she moved her finger into her mouth with his cock and slid it in and around his cock while inside her mouth. When she brought it out, she shifted her hand and became more rhythmic with the strokes of her right hand as he felt her left hand finger slowly making its way, sliding over his balls and continuing down until it reached his asshole. It was impossible to tell if he came before or after she entered him, but with every squirt of his orgasmic prick he could feel his asshole squeeze tighter and tighter against this intruder to his body. Cliff could feel Pat licking up the last remnants of his seed. She got up and left; probably to clean up. She came back, sat down and started reading her book. Cliff closed his eyes. His slightly throbbing prick was the last thing he felt as he slipped into sleep.

Cliff woke up, slowly. He looked up to see Pat standing over him.

"It's time for dinner, sleepyhead." Pat said, "How about Japanese?"

"Fine." Cliff rolled off the couch and went to the bathroom to get dressed.

After dinner, Cliff turned on the TV and Pat went into the bedroom. Cliff walked over to the bar and fixed himself a bourbon and water and settled into the couch for the night.

3 days earlier

Cliff was awake like clockwork at 6:00 am. He and Pat got up, showered and dressed by 6:45. Pat fixed scrambled eggs and biscuits for breakfast and began the lesson for the day. Cliff didn't feel like flexing his ego this morning. As was often the case, Pat had a good handle on the issues around the Israeli-Saudi negotiations, so he listened closely and took notes. Pat described the stance that he must take—negotiation above all other action. Military action would be futile; inaction would be deadly. About 9:30, he had to get started with his day.

He drove over to the Cannon House Office Building. He called Karen McCormick in to review the details that he would need for the Budget Committee meeting tomorrow. She came in with her familiar salutation, "Good morning, Representative."

Karen was wearing a grey pants suit with a white blouse that wrapped across the front rather than buttoned. Her hair was in its bun. He sat to her right so they could both read the figures and so that he could glance into her blouse when she leaned just the right way. Unfortunately, there was nothing to see. Every time she moved and displayed her chest, there was no breast to be found. "Oh well", thought Cliff, "at least she smells great."

When Cliff came out of the meeting with Karen, he had a note from Representative Knowles from Idaho. He called to see if Cliff was free for lunch. Cliff was familiar with Bob Knowles, but not friendly. Bob was also a member of the Armed Services Committee and was an outspoken hawk. Cliff thought of himself as an open-minded individual. He would listen to anyone's argument and could be persuaded by a well-reasoned approach. But when Bob took the floor, his approach to negotiations always seemed to be "shoot first and then ask, 'How did this thing start?'"

Cliff called Bob and confirmed lunch. He might as well get the name-calling out of the way at lunch rather than hear it on the Committee floor.

Lunch was all that Cliff expected. He had a turkey and cheese sandwich on a bun while listening to Representative Knowles outline his military solution to the Israel-Saudi Arabia stalemate. It included raising the readiness level of the 7th Fleet in the Indian Ocean, moving the 5th Fleet into the Mediterranean Sea and establishing a base in Jordan for the 7th Air Cavalry and the 1st Marine division whether Jordan agreed or not.

Cliff started his rebuttal. "Bob, flexing the military muscle isn't going to impress anyone. Both of those countries have been buying American armaments for years and have the most up-to-date weapons in their arsenals. The only difference between Israel and the US is that Israel has used their weapons; we haven't."

"Well, it's about time we did."

"You can't be serious. Israel is one of our strongest allies and we wouldn't be able to bring the 7th Fleet back to port if Saudi Arabia cut off our oil supply."

"Those fucking Jews are fair weather friends. They're our allies when it's to their advantage to be our allies. Like when they need money or weapons. But they're not going to stand by us when it comes to 'skin'. And I'm sick and tired of trying to deal with any of those Arabs. We've been fucked by Iraq and Iran and then every few years some religious zealot takes the stage to tell everyone that Allah told him that the US is Satan and Satan must die. What? You think the Saudis think any different because they carry cell phones around? We need to expand the borders of Idaho to include all of those oil fields and send them all to Allah."

"Look, Bob," Cliff was picking up his lunch scraps and getting ready to leave, "Let's see what we get from the talks at the table before we decide to start World War III."

"You fucking pussy, don't you know what talking brings? It brings an attack on Pearl Harbor! Yeah, that's right, Cliff. We were talking when we should have been preparing."

Cliff got up to leave. Bob continued.

"And if we don't prepare now your precious Israel is going to rip us a new asshole or maybe we'll be changing the name of Las Vegas to Mecca West."

Cliff said, "Thanks for your time." and walked away.

Bob continued; raising his voice with every step that Cliff took in the other direction, "You talking pussies are going to talk us out of the American Way of Life!"

When Cliff reached the door, he glanced back at Bob just in time to see him throw down his napkin on the table and to hear a final, "Fucking Pussy."

When he got back to the office he went into his office and closed his door. He called out to Barb to hold all calls. Cliff was a little wound up by Bob. It was so frustrating listening to right wing rhetoric, America right or wrong. As a member of the Armed Services Committee, Cliff was well aware of the Black Ops that were in constant motion. He knew very well how many people had been murdered by American Special Forces to protect the American Way of Life. But these people were murdered because they disagreed and they were vocal. Or someone thought that they might raise a group of followers or they might turn violent, or, or, or. Their fate was already decided. And some of them were Americans!

"We have to cut the cancer out wherever it exists; even in our own homes." He'd heard them say. But, what if they're right? What if they're not the cancer? What if they're innocent? Haven't we created our own Murder, Incorporated that reacts to the whim of Cliff's own constituents? How can a policy-maker like Bob Knowles be right all the time?

The field of battle has changed for America through the centuries; from face-to-face in the Revolution and Civil Wars to guerrilla tactics in the jungle. Now, we no longer burn our political enemies in ovens, we shoot them on the streets of Detroit or in apartment buildings in New York and back alleys in Paris and Baghdad.

Some days, Cliff hated this job. He leaned back in his chair and took a deep breath. He needed a release. He looked at the phone and thought about calling Cheryl. Not a good idea. Maybe Penny Johnson would come over and suck him off. Cliff laughed. He picked up the phone and called his secure voice-mail. He punched in the access code; one new message. He hit 1 for play.

"Cliff; it's Cheryl. I just wanted to leave a message to tell you that I understand that you're doing everything that you can to get me a job and if it doesn't work out, it's OK. I'm not going to worry about it. We'll find a way to be together, I know it.

And I want you to know that last Thursday was terrific. I didn't mean to spoil it this weekend and I won't do it again. Forgive me? I know you do. I love you! Try to find sometime this week. OK? Bye."

Oh God, if he could only fuck her one more time.

He picked up the phone and called Senator Golden's Office.

"This is the Office of Senator Frank Golden; how may I direct your call?"

"Penny Johnson, please."

"This is Penny."

"Penny, this is Representative Clifford Lewis."

"Oh, hi."

"Hi. I was talking to a mutual friend, Representative Baker. I was hoping that you could stop by my office when you get off work."

"Sure, no problem."

"Do you know where my office is?"

"Yeah, I'll find it."

"Great. I'll see you later then. Bring a report with you."

"Of course."

Cliff hung up the phone. He called out to Barb that Senator Golden's Office was sending a messenger with a package and she should send them in when they arrived. Otherwise, he was indisposed.

He stayed secluded in his office until late in the afternoon. Most of the staff had left by the time that Barb called. "Representative, the package has arrived from Senator Golden."

"Alright, send in the messenger. I'll need to read through the report and send a response. You can go home; I'll lock up. I don't know how long this will take."

"Very well."

There was a quick knock at the door. It opened and Barb stepped aside to let Penny walk through. Cliff looked up with the most forlorn face he could muster and said to Penny, "Please, have a seat."

"Good night, Representative." Barb called out as she closed the door.

"Good night." Cliff said as the handle clicked shut. After a few moments of shuffling in the outer room, Cliff heard the outer door shut. He stood up slowly and looked over at Penny as he walked to the door and locked it. Penny was everything that Bill had promised; pudgy little legs popping out of her short skirt, her blouse showed an extra layer of fat around her waist but it was dwarfed by the bulge that her tits made, even with half of them falling out of the top of her blouse. He walked to the couch where she was sitting. She stood up. He began unbuttoning her blouse. She tugged at his belt and was unzipping his pants by the time that he unhooked her bra and her huge breasts fell out and dangled from her chest like there was a breeze in the room. He moved to the side and sat on the couch. Penny stepped back and positioned herself on the couch with her face in his crotch but made sure that Cliff could fondle her breasts. Penny was everything that Bill had promised. She sucked him like she hadn't eaten lunch for three days. Her big nipples got as hard as he did and by the time he shot his wad, her lips were hugging his pubic hairs and the head of his prick felt like it was punching her stomach.

Cliff fell back on the couch. Penny got up, put her bra and blouse back on and While Cliff was still in recovery mode, said, "Thanks, I gotta go." And she walked to the door, unlocked it, and left, closing the door behind her. Cliff heard her footsteps and then the outer door open and close. Cliff looked down at his crotch. She'd licked it clean. That was nice. He pulled up his pants and zipped the zipper and hooked his belt closed. He went over to his desk to get his suit coat. He looked at the clock; 6:30, not too late.

Cliff got home by 7:00. Pat opened a bottle of wine and he decided to give her the Representative Knowles story in great detail. She listened intently and sipped her wine, but she didn't ask a lot of questions like she usually did. And she didn't correct him or tell him what he could have done better, like she usually did. Well, maybe he did OK.

2 days earlier

Cliff was up at 6:00 am, as usual. He showered and dressed for work and grabbed some cereal for breakfast. Pat was still acting stoned; walking around looking deep in thought but not saying anything. He left without saying 'goodbye' when he finished his cereal.

Cliff walked into his office. Barb was at her desk in the outer office.

"Good Morning, Barbara"

"Good Morning, Representative."

With that, Cliff walked into his inner office. He glanced over at the couch and thought of Penny. He'd had worse times than last night. Oh yeah, there was much worse than Penny. He laughed to himself.

But Cliff shook his head back to reality. He didn't have much time to laugh. It was Tuesday and that meant Budget Oversight Committee. Cliff smiled because it also meant Karen McCormick. And then he had to laugh at himself. What had happened to his standards? Cheryl is out of the picture and all of a sudden he's taking up with Penny and getting hot for Karen? He needed some serious ass soon or he was going to be completely out of control. He shook his head again in mock disappointment. He picked up the phone.

"Barb, call Karen and tell her to bring the files for the Budget Committee; I'll be ready to go in five minutes."

"Yes, Representative."

What the hell, they'd be in Committee all morning; he'd ask Karen to lunch, anyway.

Five minutes later he stepped out of his office. "Good morning, Representative." It was Karen. She was wearing a blue pantsuit with a white blouse buttoned to the neck. Of course, her hair was in a bun. "Good morning, Karen. Are we set?"

"Set."

Cliff took a deep breath. "Let's go". He shook his head as he followed Karen through the door. He wished that Cheryl hadn't been fired.

The Budget Committee Meeting took all morning. Karen turned him down for lunch. She had a lot of work to do from the meeting and it would take all week to be prepared for the next meeting. "Of course." said Cliff and let her off easy. He was relieved. Bun or no bun, she probably wouldn't be that good. Then she'd quit and he'd have to figure out the budget with someone less competent. It wasn't worth it. He picked up lunch along the walk back and brought it to his office. At least he bought Karen her lunch as well.

Cliff left the office just before 4:30 to give him plenty of time to get home, changed and out to the dinner. When he got home, he dropped his case by the door and walked into the Living Room to fix himself a drink. He had to do a double take when he saw, or thought he saw, Pat half-naked in the kitchen. Sure enough. He could see the bra strap and that little patch of thong just above her crack. He moved quietly into the kitchen. But when he got close, he couldn't control himself. He gave out a grunt as he grabbed her ass and grabbed it as tight as he could.

"P-l-e-a-s-e Clifford, grow up."

"What's wrong with you?"

"Nothing's wrong with me. I've had a helleva day and I don't want to talk about it. Now, let's just get dressed for dinner and get through this evening."

"Get through this evening—you make it sound like a task."

"It's work, Cliff. It's the most important work you'll do all day. It's the most important work I'll do all day."

"Yeah, yeah, yeah." Oh geez, the bitch was back. Cliff ran off to the shower and went into the bedroom and turned on the TV while Pat walked into the bathroom. He walked out to the Living Room to finish getting the drink that he never got to and dressed as he watched TV and drank his bourbon.

Pat came out dressed almost like a man. Cliff shook his head and put on his jacket. Cliff could tell it was going to be one of those nights; Pat would be walking around wishing she had a dick and acting like she did. He was going to have to peel off from her as soon as they hit the dinner.

Sure enough, as soon as they were passed the greeting line, Cliff went looking for anyone else but Pat. He found Bill Baker first.

"Cliff, how's everything?"

"Everything's out of control. I'm out of control."

"You called Penny didn't you?"

"Yeah."

"You dog."

"You're calling me a dog? Penny's a dog."

"Well, we all have our talents. We don't all have looks." Trying to change the subject, Bill said, "What's on the agenda tonight?"

"I don't know, but it must be big. Did you see Pat?"

"No, why?"

"Well, I think that I'll be accused of being a homosexual unless she takes off her clothes and proves that she's a woman."

Bill laughs. "She just wants to be one of the guys."

"Yeah! I think it's time to pick our table and begin the speeches. Let's see who Pat has put us near. See you later. Wish me luck."

"Luck has nothing to do with it; it's all pre-meditated."

Bill was right. Pat always had someone at the table that she planned on charming throughout dinner and even onto the dance floor, if they resisted. But not tonight. When Cliff joined Pat at the table she had selected he didn't see anyone of recent importance. And Pat didn't seem overly interested in anyone in particular as the dinner was served. By the time the speeches had started, Cliff was sure that something had gone wrong. Pat wasn't more than polite to everyone at the table, including him. No grilling anyone; no sweet talk; nothing but everyday chit-chat with everyone at the table.

The President started in with his EAT program. Cliff had heard this song before; an obvious re-election ploy. Pat seemed to be interested, so he took the opportunity to look around the room and see who else looked interesting. He didn't see much, a lot of the same faces that you see at these dinners. But then, about five tables over was a nice blond who seemed to have been very interested in the President's speech but started looking around the room when Chairman Russell took the mike. Maybe she was into power. He'd have to check her out later. Good old Chairman Russell, he was off making the same threats that he always made in Committee but with a little more tact and a little less sweat and spitting.

When the music started, Cliff was a little surprised when Chairman Russell walked over and asked Pat for a dance. Now the evening was beginning to come into focus. Pat was going to try to calm the beast that was the head of the Armed Services Committee, save the country and somehow pass the glory over to him. Wonderful! At least he knew what to expect. A few minutes after the dance, Pat would step away and she'd have her talk with the Chairman, probably the same one that he'd already heard a hundred times. 'We can't piss off Israel; we can't piss off Saudi Arabia; let's just arbitrate this thing and be done with it. Let's put away the swords and pull up our chairs until it's resolved.'

Good luck. Anyway, Cliff could use the time to meet the 21st Century's Marilyn Monroe over there.

He waited patiently while Pat danced. She came back and sat down without a word. A few minutes and a few sips of her drink later, she said, "I have to go to the Ladies Room." Cliff nodded his head as she started towards the back of the room. Once she was out of the room, Cliff picked up his drink and began walking around the tables in the direction of Marilyn. He waited a few minutes; a couple of tables away as the man that he assumed was her date got caught up in a conversation and slowly drifted away from the table. Marilyn looked a little uncomfortable at being left alone and started looking around the room. When her eyes fell on Cliff, he raised his glass in a toast. Marilyn smiled, picked up her drink and made her way over to Cliff. As she got close she raised her glass and said, "Cheers."

"Cheers. I'm Representative Clifford Lewis and you are?"

"Ready for this night to end."

"Not exactly what you thought it was going to be?"

"Not at all. I thought that I'd meet the President. That's what Dick told me. It was a great speech but I can't get near him. Look, he's completely surrounded by those secret service guys or whatever."

"What's your name?"

"Huh?"

"What's your name?"

"Oh, I'm sorry, Marilyn, Marilyn Brewster.

'Of course' Cliff thought. "How about if I take you over there and introduce you to the President? Would that help your evening?"

"Are you kidding me? That would be unbelievable. Can you really do that?"

"C'mon, let's see." Cliff took her hand and glided her towards the President. The Secret Service agents parted at his arrival and he brought Marilyn up to the edge of the table. Cliff tipped his head slightly to the President and said, "Mr. President, I would like to introduce you to Marilyn Brewster. Marilyn is a great fan of yours, but a little shy. So, I told her that I would make the introductions."

The President stood up and shook Marilyn's hand and said, "Please, don't be shy. It's a pleasure to meet you."

Marilyn stammered, "I loved your speech."

The President looked at her with appreciation and said, "Then we have something in common; I did too."

Someone leaned over the table and whispered something to the President. His attention had moved on and Marilyn seemed OK with making an exit at that point.

Marilyn was most appreciative for meeting the President. She and Cliff chatted for a while and finally agreed to meet again next Tuesday after work for a drink. Cliff gave Marilyn his message phone number and explained that it was completely secure and that only he will hear the messages. Marilyn was obviously impressed and slipped the paper into her cleavage. Cliff noticed that Pat was back at the table. She hadn't noticed him yet. He thanked Marilyn for the conversation and reminded her of their drink next Tuesday. She would be there.

Cliff made his way back to the table and sat down next to Pat.

"What's wrong? You don't look so good."

"I don't feel so good. Can we go home?"

Cliff's mission was accomplished; he was shuttling Pat out of there a minute later.

1 day earlier

Cliff was up at 6:00 am, as usual. Pat wasn't budging and he wasn't going to wake a sleeping lioness. He made some coffee and warmed a bagel and found the cream cheese in the refrigerator. He checked the bedroom just before leaving. Pat almost had an eye open. He told her that he had eaten and that he was leaving. She mumbled a few incomprehensible words as Cliff walked out the door.

The office was quiet. He focused on the mail and getting caught up on all those responses that he needed to do for political reasons. For him, those were always the first to be put aside and the last to be picked up again.

He thought little of Cheryl. Once the thought entered his head to check with Bill on the Justice job, but he discarded it almost as quickly as it had come in. He didn't want to bother Bill with a lost cause.

Cliff came home. Pat was set on going out for Italian food. They went to D'Amore. Pat ordered a bottle of Santa Margherita Pinot Grigio. She was an absolute pig. Cliff had never seen her put so much food and drink away in one sitting. She ate the appetizers, the dinner, the dessert and drained the bottle of wine as she went through it all. Cliff thought that she had decided to forgo her figure and just put on weight. On the way back home he commented, "I've never seen you eat like that before; appetizers and desert. What's up?"

"Nothing", she said with her Cheshire smile, "I was just hungry."

That was wonderful, now his wife was going to become a blimp.

Today

Cliff was finally starting to settle into a more normal routine. Pat was up early with him; fixed him breakfast and seemed almost happy as she saw him off to work. He strolled into his office without the immediate pressure of major concerns from one or more of his Committees. He leisurely said good morning to Barbara and settled into his office mail with a fresh cup of coffee.

About 10:00 he started over to the Capitol for a discussion by the Agriculture Committee regarding the declining price of beef. Normally, he left this type of meeting to his staffers, and he was sure one would be there, but he wanted to be a part of the discussion and make a point to his 'cattle constituents' that he had been there for them. On the way, he met Representative Cohen from New York. He knew Alvin from the AS Committee but wanted to get a little closer to the Representative. After a few minutes of chit-chat, they broke off with Representative Cohen calling back, "See you on Monday."

Cliff was a little taken aback, "Monday?"

"Yeah, the AS Committee is back on starting Monday at 8:00".

"I haven't gotten any word."

Representative Cohen shrugged his shoulders with his arms flapping out slightly and a frown on his face.

"OK", said Cliff, "See you Monday."

"Bye."

Cliff made it to the Ag Meeting just a little late and took copious notes but no motions were brought and no changes were put in place, so Cliff went back to his office. He'll have to talk to Pat about these issues. She'll know the approach to take with the voters.

When he got back to the office, there was a message of a party caucus meeting tomorrow morning. Damn, this was always bad news. It meant a shake-up by the brass. People moving from one Committee to another as the pecking order changed for whatever reason.

Cliff left the office at five o'clock and went straight to the apartment. He didn't tell Pat anything about the caucus meeting. He didn't want to hear all of the bad political signs that this meant, and how he must have fucked up somewhere along the line; how he was to act at the meeting, blah, blah, blah.

Pat was sweet when he got home. Not demonstrative, not loving, not caring, but sweet. Cliff was feeling that there was reason for concern.

The day after

Pat was up early this morning and fixed breakfast for Cliff. He didn't explain why he had to be in the office early today. Pat didn't even press the issue.

He had to be at the Caucus Meeting at 8:00am. They always tried to get these things over before the day got going. He entered the Caucus Room and thought he must have been in the wrong room or way too early. Only the Whip, Representative Clarence Carter and the Majority Leader, Senator Edward Jefferson were present. As soon as he sat in a chair near the two men, Clarence began the conversation—soliloquy is more like it.

"Cliff, we're going to make a few changes in the Committee assignments. We're relieving you of your AS and Budget responsibilities and assigning you to Education and Land Management. We'll get you the schedules and send some staffers from the Committee Chairmen's offices to bring your staffers up to date."

At that, Senator Jefferson stood up, walked over to Cliff with an outstretched hand and said, "Cliff." Cliff shook his hand, he thought. By now, Representative Carter was on his feet with his hand out, "Thanks, Cliff." Cliff seemed to shake his hand too, and then he was alone.

Cliff wandered back to his office by 10:00 am. He was still dazed when Barbara called through the fog and caught his attention.

"Representative, I think Cheryl Chapin is missing."

"What?"

"Cheryl Chapin, she worked at ICC." Barbara said for the benefit of anyone else who might be listening. "Robert Williams the 3rd called looking for her. She didn't come into work today. He's contacted everyone looking for her. He thinks she's disappeared. He even went to her apartment. It was locked and no one has seen her this morning. No one saw her leave for work."

"Have the police been contacted."

"Yes, but she's an adult and can't be listed as missing until 24 hours have passed since someone last saw her."

"When did someone see her?"

"When she left work last night; Robert said that he was going to file a report at 5 o'clock this afternoon and join the police when they entered her apartment."

"OK, well there doesn't seem to be anything else to do. She may just be out and around."

"I don't think so. It's not like her. I'm worried."

"Please don't worry. I'm sure it will all turn out alright."

Barb stood with her mouth open as Cliff went into his office. She didn't seem consoled. In fact, she looked a little pissed. What did she expect? He can't go running around the city looking for her. Pat's still in town.

Pat! Damn, how was he going to explain how he got his ass kicked today? And he didn't even know why. He needed some help.

He picked up the phone and dialed.

"This is the Office of Senator Frank Golden; how may I direct your call?"

"Penny Johnson, please."

"This is Penny."

"Penny, this is Representative Clifford Lewis." Silence.

"Do you think you could stop by my office this afternoon?"

"I'm sorry, I'm leaving town this weekend and I need to get packed and ready."

"I see. Well, maybe some other time, then." Silence.

"Good bye." The line disconnected.

Cliff was furious. Even that fucking whore wouldn't touch him. What was going on? He had become untouchable almost overnight.

Cliff left his office early. He looked at Barb as he walked by. Her eyes were wet and puffed.

"Still no word from Cheryl." She said.

"Good night." Cliff said and kept walking.

When he got home, he was in no mood to go to a State Dinner, but Pat was dressed and ready to go. She said they had to go.

He told her about the Caucus Meeting this morning, hoping that she'd get pissed off and they wouldn't have to go to the Dinner. But she didn't go ballistic. In fact she said that that was even more reason to go to the Dinner tonight. Let the party brass know what he's made of.

What kind of bullshit was that? His status just took a huge hit and most likely his career was in a tail-spin, which meant that her career was in a tail-spin, and she gives him the old 'pull yourself up by the bootstraps' talk. What the fuck was going on?

They went to the dinner. Cliff felt like a leper and acted accordingly. He wasn't sure because he never paid attention to Pat at any of the previous dinners, but she seemed to enjoy herself more than she did at the others. He sat alone and drank. She flitted from one conversation to another; giggling here and looking serious there. Finally, they left.

At home, Pat went to the bathroom and went to bed. Cliff stayed up and finished the bourbon.

The second day after

Pat had left early for the airport and her trip back home. Cliff stayed in the apartment, not even going to the office as he had done so many other Saturday mornings.

Just after noon, he received a call from a reporter with the *Post*. "Exactly what was the nature of your relationship with Cheryl Chapin?"

"I knew her because she was from my District. I considered her a friend."

"A good friend?"

"I don't understand the question."

"We have reason to believe that your relationship may have been more intimate than simply 'friends'. Do you wish to comment on that?"

"I have nothing more to say."

"Do you know where Ms. Chapin is right now?"

"No, I don't. Good Bye."

There were three more calls with similar content during the afternoon. Cliff decided to stop answering the phone. He sat in disbelief. What had happened to his life? It was all so surreal. And what did Cheryl's disappearance have to do with him? Where could he turn? Pat seemed distant when she left. Where else could he get information?

Maybe Cheryl left a message for him. He called for his phone messages. There were three; one from Wednesday, one from Thursday and one earlier today. Cheryl! He hit the code to play the messages.

"Cliff, Cheryl. Hey babe, I guess I'm not going to get that Justice job and I haven't heard anything from State although I've followed up everyday. Anyway, I'll be making my arrangements to go back home tomorrow. I've got to leave by the weekend so I can start looking for a job in Phoenix on Monday. I really want to see you before I go. Send me a message. OK? I love you. I miss you."

"Cliff, it's lonely Cheryl. I have a flight to Phoenix on Saturday. I leave at 11:05 AM. That leaves us about 30 hours to get together. I swear, I think I'll bust if I don't see you. So, help a girl out, OK? I love you."

"Representative Lewis, this is Marilyn Brewster. I'm not going to be able to make it on Tuesday. I know you'll understand."

978-0-595-47809
0-595-47809-3

Printed in Great Britain
by Amazon

50544049R00080